A LIFE OF STAR LIBRARIES
Gruppo A.V. Italia S.r.l.
VAT no. 03624001206
COPYRIGHT FRANCESCA TERRAZZINO

O5 NOVEMBER 2022, BOLOGNA

english

The Paradigm of Vanilla's Option

The Paradigm of Vanilla's Option

This novel is a work of fiction.
Names, characters, places and events are either figments of the
author's imagination or used fictitiously.
Any resemblance to real places or events or to real or existing
persons is unintentional and purely coincidental.
All rights reserved. No part of this volume may be reproduced,
stored or transmitted in any form or by any means, electronic,
mechanical, photocopying, disk or otherwise, including film, radio,
television, without written permission of the publisher.
Reproductions made for professional, economic or commercial
purposes or in any case for use other than personal use may be made
following specific authorisation by,

A life of star libraries,
Gruppo A.V. Italia S.r.l.
VAT no. 03624001206
05 November 2022

__To Anna and Viola__

__incontrovertible parameters__

__of the dream__

THE PARADIGM OF VANILLA'S OPTION

FRANCESCA TERRAZZINO

The Paradigm of Vanilla's Option

By the same author

Noi fantasmi non ascoltiamo che il nostro passato (2003)

Equilibrio liquido (2019)

Tacit assonances (2021) vers It. En. Es. Fr.

Black red white blood (2022) vers. It. En. Es. Fr.

The Paradigm of Vanilla's Option

Chapter One

The room was dark, seemingly empty except for a small blue plastic child's chair in its centre.

It was illuminated by a light from the roof.

He approached the chair with an overwhelming desire to sit on it, even though it was infinitely larger. It was one of those Ikea chairs found in nurseries or kindergartens, gathered around colourful tables and on the walls, drawings of illiterate children who unconditionally love life.

He sat down, staring at the ceiling.

This opened like the sunroof of a car, gradually revealing a clear blue sky, an intense sun, probably summer, and a few clouds streaked with white that sporadically, driven by the wind, crossed the view.

He heard an animal cry in the distance, high-pitched and shrill, coming from the open hatch, from that summer sky, again and again screeching the air like worn car brakes, like tracks under the insistent pressure of the rails, like a bird flying and calling out to its fellows, guiding them in the ancestral shifting of the nest. The view of the blue quickly clouded over from a wingspan of at least four metres, passed over and disappeared, bringing the sun back to its brilliance, passed over his face and disappeared, blinding him again.

He passed and passed many times over many birds who now called each other.

Their long beaks, their featherless wings, their large wingspans, gave him the impression that they were not common birds, common in that world, in that era, in that millennium.

He gathered his arms, hugging himself tightly, an icy air flooded the room, small snowflakes flashed near him, the light dimmed, the wind howled as in blizzards, the temperature dropped several degrees. His teeth flapped violently against each other, his body trembled, but he remained motionless on that little blue child's chair, in the centre of a dimly lit room with nothing but him and that glimpse of the world curtained by his ceiling.

The Paradigm of Vanilla's Option

A few minutes, a blinding sun returned, African heat, drops of sweat beaded his forehead, roaring n the distance.

"I want to get up," he proclaimed loudly.

His body obeyed, he got up from his seat.

"I want to leave this room"

His legs moved towards what now appeared to be a door.

"I want to open the door"

His hand grasped the lock that was not there before, gripped it and squeezed it tightly, lowering it and pushing to get out, to return to before.

'The door opens'

The door gave way.

He saw his room, a sigh of relief calmed him.

"I want to go to my bed"

Her body moved, and she recomposed herself in the double bed, with the blankets unmade and dishevelled, vaguely smelling of sweat and saltiness, a symptom of infrequent washing and many sleepless nights in which her body had tossed and turned in them.

He lay down, closed his eyes and prone with his hands clasped on his chest said aloud, "I want to wake up".

He blinked hard.

He remained motionless, absorbing all the noises in the room, all the smells, all the sensations he could grasp in the silence and darkness of the stillness.

Nothing, the silence of the night enveloped him. He moved his head slightly, raising it slowly, observing his room.

A desk cluttered with papers, a plasma TV, an open wardrobe laden with crumpled clothes. Shoes on the floor, a wooden chair, entirely covered by several woollen jackets.

A bedside table with some medicines and a yellowed glass of water.

An unlit abat jour. The window open, the curtains moved by a light night breeze, the moonlight gently invading the room.

He was at home, he was back.

He looked at his hands, he had to have definitive proof.

He tried to insert his right index finger into the palm of his left hand.

The fingertip met the flesh and stopped.

He was awake.

"What a fucking trip this time!"

He pulled himself up from the covers, the bed creaked.

He went to his PC, turned it on, retrieved the unfinished file, wrote

Lucid dream 22, I find myself for an estimated time of twenty minutes in prehistory. I left at 3.06 and returned at 4.22. To return I gave orders to my body in a loud voice. Notes: the body reacted to the stresses of cold and heat as if it were real. My shirt is still soaked with sweat, the sweat caused by the increased temperature of the dream.

Before leaving, I had planned to see my childhood, so I totally missed out.

He picked up his mobile phone, it was almost empty, to be charged he mentally recorded, he could dial the number and hope for an orthodox call.

"It's me, were you asleep?"

A woman's voice greeted him.

"Of course, it's night"

"I wanted to say goodbye, I miss you"

"You don't and please stop phoning us at night, I always think it's the phone call from the police or the hospital informing me of your death, but instead I'm disappointed and it's you!"

"Don't be like that...everything will change and I will finally be able to please you and fulfil all your and Gio's wishes, how is he? Is he asleep? Is he asking for me?"

"No, he doesn't ask for you, he's ashamed and says he has no father to his friends, he just wants to forget, just like me...and then I'm not alone...please stop calling me..."

"You are not alone? Are you? Who is it? It touches you...yes it definitely touches you...please, I love you! Give me another chance! I'll solve everything for our family, for the three of us!"

Silence.

The line had been interrupted.

Francis looked at his hands. They were trembling slightly. A small, timid tear slipped down his cheek and fell into nothingness.

He got up from his chair, he had lost a lot of weight, he had eaten intermittent meals and fast food. He should have shaved, maybe washed, combed his hair. He looked around the room, a resounding disaster.

He walked over to the poster of Brook Shield in Blue Lagoon, caressed the actress' youthful face, her full mouth, her swollen lips, her wavy brown hair falling softly over her bare shoulders. He became aroused.

"Baby, you believe me true...I'm going to make it, I'm going to get everything I want and I'm going to share it with you, my baby" She demurely slid her hand over her breasts barely covered by her swimming costume, caressed the skin that remained bare and followed the contours on the coloured bra, that little blue triangle that little could cover of that exuberant teenage breast.

The other hand went to his member, shining inside his faded pyjamas. He released it and quickly reached orgasm.

"Baby, only you can make me come like this, I love you so much, you are my only companion"

He decided to wash himself quickly, then threw himself onto the battered blankets and let a restful sleep catch him.

Brooke seemed to blink disconsolately but motherly at her dreamless sleep.

Claudia also winked at her American coffee served in the classic cardboard box with a plastic lid to retain its heat and aroma. She had the first shift that week, hoping the market would behave well and not force her into exhausting labours to cover loss-making assets.

Financier, graduated cum laude, shamelessly salaried by Private Banking Assurance for whom she managed six-figure clients in a boutique buy-and-hold business including often profitable Vanilla Options. A small banking boutique, Milanese, active in the insurance business. A business indeed that could not fall, profits were steady, registering up to +3% in a net month.

After deducting taxes at 26%, there was a very interesting capital left and she was working on a fixed and commission basis ... ergo she was really getting rich.

The Paradigm of Vanilla's Option

She looked absentmindedly at her Prada shoes, a gift from S&P, cream, shiny, refined pumps with a ten-centimetre heel that would sometimes displace customers.

Yet if one reached his level, necessarily elegance and charm had to be acquired and mastered.

She straightened her long brown hair, which fell in soft waves, her face wide, her blue eyes intense, veiled by soft black lashes. She vaguely resembled a bygone actress, who was for two generations past a true sex symbol, debuting with only one truly successful film, Blue Lagoon.

Certainly his older clients did not fail to remind him of this, he did not wish to imagine what adolescent dreams they might have harboured in the silence of their little rooms, imagining themselves with the sinful teenager in the film.

She wore a soft silk dress, a champagne-coloured trouser suit, fastened at the waist, frivolously revealing a fuchsia top that barely covered her ample breasts.

The combination of deference and rebellion, of order and liveliness, masculinity and sensuality intrigued her almost as much as the adrenalin caused by a good deal. The violent pulsing of the blood in the veins of her neck as she watched the histograms go up, the numbers go down, the synapses processing fast, injecting compensatory hormones, intensifying the probabilistic possibility that reasoning was winning. A few seconds to decide whether to lose money or gain it.

She won.

For this they paid her well and she could afford to be beautiful and seductive even in front of the most important and conservative clients, at least as long as she brought in major increases. After that, ignominy and nothingness.

"Claudia, good morning, your turn this morning?"

The caretaker turned his usual beaming smile on her.

"Yes Antonio, thank you, will you open?"

The double doors opened, the infrared registered that she was not carrying any weapons or dangerous objects, and the green light gave her the go-ahead to enter the financial inner sanctum.

A small trading room surrounded by active monitors with indices, numbers and charts, three chairs, a gargoyle of fresh water.

Essential.

"Good morning!" pronounced the beautiful Claudia to the empty room.

Chapter Two

Francis rose on the coming day, it was July, perhaps, on an unspecified day.

Zero food in the fridge, zero clean clothes, zero matching socks.

He decided to start working immediately, Brooke had given him new vigour.

Lucid dream number 23, I imagine myself navigating through a mountain of real money, 50 euro notes, a real mountain. I imagine that I always did that even when I was a child, I imagine me, a child, navigating through a mountain of 50 euro money. I imagine my family, together with me, sailing in a mountain of real money, driving luxury cars, lots of Ferraris, and living in a castle! I imagine all this to rebuild my paradigm. To restructure the subconscious and recreate in reality, part of the lucid dream.

I start to think about it now, I get into the armchair and think about it going into tranche. It's about 11 o'clock, it's morning, I haven't eaten or drunk but I have slept peacefully without dreams for about five hours.

He got up from the PC, heading for the armchair, into which he sank with a light breath from his body.

She closed her eyes and imagined a child figure with her mind's eye.

He was smaller in size, but still him, his skin smoother, he already wore glasses (*note in the lucid dream imaginings of a child as a representation of the mini-adult, even with glasses, belly and baldness)* he was led by hand by his mother. She loved him, caressed his chubby cheeks affectionately.

His mother drove a silver Bentley, she was a beautiful and refined woman, she would get him into the car, fasten his seat belt, and tell him that they were going for a short ride and that he would have a good time. It would be like going to Disneyworld and going down a rollercoaster.

He nodded, happy to see a beautiful and charming mother.

The car had started with a dulcet roar of the powerful engine, they soon entered a long, dimly lit tunnel, speeding past a series of trucks.

He had to do the test of dreaming, (*always remember to immediately rehearse staying in the lucid dream)* he inserted the index finger of his right hand into the palm of his right hand. The index finger effortlessly penetrated the matter, sticking out the other end of the hand.

OK we're in!

The tunnel opened onto an immense cavern, as high as a Ferris wheel and enclosed in every direction. Headlights hanging from the side of the walls illuminated a single spot.

They approached with the car, right in the centre of the cave, in the only lit spot. The car stopped, Francis the child got out, followed by his mother. In front of him was a small mound of 50 euro banknotes, about the same height as him. Next to it, another pyramid of the same height of 24-carat gold bars. In the last mound, gold coins, antique and rough minted.

The child Francis threw himself onto the mound of banknotes, soft and fragrant like a good, cosy mattress. He smelled it, the magnanimous odour of wealth, inhaled it at the top of his lungs with his nostrils immersed in the vivid and intense aroma of money.

He turned around and turned the 50 euro pieces inside out, taking them in his hand, checking their authenticity and watermark, he passed them over his face, over his body, laughing out loud for a child still full of innocence.

Then he woke up slightly and approached the brightness emanating from the gold bars. As he approached his ears came a dense, deep bell noise. A single beat as if they were ancient Tibetan bells, followed by a deep, baritone chant OMMMM. Again, bell, OMMMM, bell, OMMMM...he could not remember having had any experience of Buddhist prayer, neither as a child nor as an adult.

(mark enters a promiscuous element whose origin we do not know).

"I think I should share this wealth with someone."

He imagined another person getting out of the car.

A sinuous and beautiful woman, sweet and yielding.

The door opened, lust took hold of him completely, a woman's leg appeared, veiled by black tights, a prominent heel enhanced her slender ankles, then another leg came down, then her body and face. It was his ex-wife.

She approached him as a child. She looked at him contemptuously and darkly.

"You stupid wormy being, these are mine! You owe them to me to raise the abortion you conceived with me and who unfortunately resembles you. The abortion that will become a loser like you and that I still can't get away from you..."

(wake up now, IMMEDIATELY, the dream derails)

"No they are mine, go away you hag, I loved you, you betrayed me with a beggar for a few pennies, they are mine and my son's, or maybe to win you back, you, my life, my honour..." the last words were lost in a sob, Francis covered his face, curled up in the mountain of banknotes and wept.

The mother approached, "My little one, you have always been a landslide, even when you couldn't speak, everything was difficult, you are difficult, you can never do what you want, because your paradigm is this, look at yourself, look at little Francis..."

The money was gone, he was in a small, cramped kitchenette, a pot was boiling with an egg inside. Greasy tea towels were hanging from a wooden chair.

A table with an absurd plastic tablecloth read "Good morning, it's Sunday!" at every 10 cm by 10 cm square, winking an abominable eye enclosed in a cappuccino cup.

The eye looked at Francis, "Little one, Good morning! It's Sunday, wake up or it will be tarsi and the dream will eat you!"

The saucepan with the boiling water inside, began to mumble fiercely, the four burners of the old white ceramic stove lit, they were gas-powered, they ignited and burned, raising their flames to the maximum.

A small chair approached Francis from behind and took him to sit down, caught him all over with its enveloping arms, crawling towards the fires. The tablecloth intoned, "Francis eats the egg that is ready!" the small chair crawled closer and closer to the burning fires, impossible to escape.

"I want to wake up! I WANT TO WAKE UP NOW'

The fire faded, the chair let go, his mother entered the kitchen.

"You see him playing with fire, what happens? You pulled your hair tight..."

Francis opened his eyes, he was an adult, in the silence of his room, on the armchair. He opened his eyes and remained motionless, as if waking from nightmares.

In his hands he held a 50 euro note, clutched like an oar for a castaway.

The light was still daylight. He moved his eyes, he was home.

He had to be sure.

He pointed the index finger of his right hand into the palm of his left hand. The index finger crashed into the palm. He had to cut his nails.

He was at home, he was awake, he had 50 Euros in his hand.

He stood up.

"Brooke, my love, my beloved goddess, the lean cows are over, I did it! I'll buy you whatever you want!"

He headed for the computer.

The Paradigm of Vanilla's Option

Lucid dream number 23. Strongly unstable, the subconscious betrayed me, childhood came back to haunt me but I brought the note with me. More autosuggestion over the subconscious, hypnosis to forget the past.

He only had to check one fact, got up, went to the mirror.

A few hairs on the left temple were pulled back.

"No matter, no matter, today I got the first real result, I just have to stabilise with hypnosis, the past. And forget the paradigm. Build a new paradigm and the subconscious will react differently."

He turned to Brooke, "Honey, I'm doing this for you...soon I'll really have you and you'll be mine like Ferraris, riches, I'll bring everything from here. Everything!"

Claudia got up from her chair, what a busy morning: the S&P 500 index was down three points, the Euro Stoxx 50 had stabilised, the Nasdaq went up. She should have covered. Enough now. She stood up, unzipped her suit jacket, she needed air, the adrenalin was still rushing through her body. She needed vitamin D, sunlight, watching the sun, balancing the hormones in her system.

"I'm going for a walk, here at lunchtime we know that nothing happens, in the afternoon we'll see."

"OK Clo, see you later, bring me a long coffee."

From his seat, Henry winked at her politely. He was the eldest of the group, and it was extremely difficult for him to imagine that women could speak in public, drive cars and even have the right to educate themselves, speak and vote. But he was a distinguished and very kind man.

She heard him reach for her "If you don't cover, you're in trouble, come back soon miss..."

Right, just air, sun, food and water. The necessary to think reasonably and reflect the best solution.

He headed for the usual bar. He crossed the street as usual, the bistro was full of noisy people, he looked for a sheltered corner.

He chose a small, round, two-seater table, at its centre the paper napkins in the container provided and a small ashtray. On the table the sticker with the Qr code to scan for the menu. He knew it by heart and had little imagination about food.

The waiter in his usual trousers, white shirt and worn tennis shoes approached.

"Francesco, here it is, I'm in a bit of a hurry. A toast, a juice with ice, a half-caf and a long coffee to go"

Francis stared at her. She was as beautiful as ever, his Brooke.

Chapter Three

The order came quickly, the toast was cold, the fontina cheese still partly frozen, the juice without ice and the half-carbonated, hot.

"Impeccable service as always...'

"You know I don't know your name..." he turned to her.

"I honestly thought you didn't speak, after years I find out now that you speak and you are of this world!"

He chuckled, his face turned red.

"Sorry, I didn't mean to disturb you, you're always in a hurry."

"Yeah right, today too, so excuse me I have to go, how much is the bill, I'll leave it with you with the tip, OK?"

"No no miss, it's on me, when I can, I would like to tell you a fact."

"Thank you Francesco, but I have to go back now"

"Tomorrow?"

"Are you serious?"

"Yes Miss..." Claudia observed him, probably for the first time, in his face. His eyes sunken in, his beard a few days old, white with dark circles under his eyes, sparse hair that concentrated on his temples to thin out hopelessly on his skull. He had a double chin and jowly cheeks, but he didn't look bad, just forlorn.

"What do you want to propose to me? An unbreakable bargain?"

He stretched his lips and began a little dance, balancing his weight from his left foot to his right.

'A bargain, yes'

"Francis...excuse me I am constantly being offered business of all kinds and magnitudes, will I be able to do them all? Will they all be profitable? Maybe not...I'm wasting my time, excuse me I have to go. Takeaway coffee?"

"Miss, you think you are on autopilot in your business. You order, and it happens."

"You can't!"

"Yet ..."

"You don't convince me..."

Claudia had stood up, trying to move without touching him to gain the exit. She was very annoyed.

"The S&P dropped 3 points today, didn't it?"

"Yeah, what do you know about that?" she looked at her Prada pumps for a second, the investors were going to call her soon.

'Tomorrow it goes up by 5'

"Maybe...then it goes down, it's finance. That's how it works."

"Tomorrow it goes up by five," he turned and left.

Claudia shook her head, she could no longer come to that bar.

He went through the door and returned to his post, he had obviously forgotten the coffee for Henry.

Francis was very shaken. He had to get home quickly and get that index finger up, he had not been able to resist, he had dared, now if he wanted to keep the advantage of curiosity, he would have to be consistent with his claims.

In two hours he would have finished his shift, hurry up, time is running out in my favour.

He had to be precise he could not allow the subconscious to enter his dream. He had to start the hypnosis now. He put on his headphones and switched on the audio from his mobile phone. Music at 528

MHZ began to play inside him. He turned the audio down slightly to hear the customers' orders, he would have to be content. Along with the music, in the distance, very faintly, his recorded voice repeated motivating phrases.

I am positive energy.

I am a constructive force.

I can realise my dreams.

I forget the past.

The past flows away from me like river water.

I earn money in increasing amounts according to continuous flows from multiple sources.

I am positive energy.

I am a constructive force.

I can realise my dreams.

I forget the past.

The past flows away from me like river water.

I earn money in increasing amounts according to continuous flows from multiple sources.

The hours passed quickly.

"Claudia, I have the Lawyer on the line, shall I put him through?"

"Of course Enrico, I'll take it in the conference room though, please."

"Yes of course, go on, I'll put him through."

"Avvocato Adolfi, good evening."

"What happened today? I'll be brief, give me your strategy and I'll leave you right away."

"I hedged with the Nasdaq. The loss is small'

"How much?"

"1 million 583 thousand euro and 20 cents"

Silence.

"She is the best. Don't let me down," and hung up.

Claudia stayed a few minutes with the phone in her hand, she was stunned.

In the end she was a woman, don't let me down...an absent father, the desire to be good, non-existent boyfriends, a child mother and knowledge as power, as redemption, as a token to be good, the best.

And then don't let me down ... and again be a woman on the eve of graduation, on the eve of a life that perhaps could have been different with other paradigms, a loving father, money for herself, a loving mother, sisters or brothers, uncles who bought her ice cream on the playground, friends who teased her a little.

He returned to the trading room. The monitors had stopped, the day was over.

"Henry you know that before declaring war, the Romans relied on the predictions of the gods, watched the entrails of cattle, the flight of birds, if a raven appeared at their door or worse still, an owl, an omen of death."

"What are you getting at? To have your palm read to figure out what to do tomorrow?" Enrico smiled, stress had won the girl over.

"No, or almost, in the end maybe you can never really predict what will happen, the variables are multiple, when added up they zero out, yet this does not happen, one always prevails over the others."

"You know what to do, you've really always done very well, you have to trust your chances."

Her eyes glazed slightly at those kind words.

"An insignificant man told me today that the S&P will go up five tomorrow, as if he had a crystal ball or read in coffee grounds. But if that were the case, really, like a prediction or the crow flapping its wings five times instead of ten, or flying left instead of right, this Henry, would really mean that we are just meat at the mercy of entropy, of absolute and debilitating disorder, restless and invincible."

"I think invincible is correct, yes."

"I'm going home now"

"I find it a very good idea, dear, tomorrow you will be victorious, you will see, I will close, go"

"Thank you"

And she headed out to the quietness of home.

Francis urinated, said goodbye to Brooke and settled into his chair.

Lucid dream 24. The goal is very simple, I have to imagine the graphs, visualise them and make them go up, just one, as if I myself were the builder, saw them and could put one brick on top of another and build a 5-storey skyscraper. A five-storey skyscraper.

I can.

He was an adult in this dream, grown up and very muscular, handsome, taller, with hair, brown, flowing, with a beautiful forelock falling partly over his forehead.

He wore a clean white shirt with his initials embroidered on the left wrist. Beige linen trousers and a jacket, also linen, beige open. He was slim. He smiled contentedly, he was a handsome, admiring man. A few women passing in the street pointed to him, smiling, imagining they were chosen for a night of fiery love.

She wore a small diamond earring on her right earlobe, sparkling in the light. He had always longed for a small diamond earring, like rich men, suddenly enriched, exploiting ease as they inhale air, voraciously, quickly, eagerly.

He should have verified that he was in the dream. But if it had been reality, it would have lasted forever.

(imposing verification)

He brought his right index finger to his left palm, his finger crossed it.

(do not be distracted from the task, even if the dream is pleasant)

He turned around, saw the graphs, they were really huge, all around him, as one on top of the other they were below him, above him, in three dimensions, he himself now had no floor, no north, no south.

'I want a compass'

From his jacket pocket, he pulled out a small compass, the needle marked north. He followed it, the diagrams reassembled in a straight line.

"I am looking for the S&P"

The monthly chart of the index came into view.

"I want to see the daily chart"

He changed his view, the descent of the index was now clear. Francis headed for the last histogram, it was red. About as high as he was.

'I want more light'

A crystal-clear light illuminated the room, there were no boundaries, the other graphics were confined, blurred to the edges of his personal trading room.

'I want to photocopy the last value'

The last value appeared before him, identical to the previous one.

"Now I want it to rise and turn green, it must rise one point at 10.00 A.M."

"I want one more, it has to rise one more point at 10.01 A.M."

"I want three more, they have to rise one point +1, each at 10.02, 10.03, 10.04, 10.05 respectively, and then stabilise on the rise all day."

The index followed the order and drew its green curve upwards until 6pm in the evening.

A long trail of unmistakable greens.

He caressed them, they were his salvation, his ticket to eternal happiness.

"Now I want to fuck, I am happy and beautiful"

One of the parallelepipeds quickly transformed into a racy brunette, with large breasts barely covered by a small red dress. One could almost glimpse the areola of the rosy nipple.

Life was beautiful.

(remember, I like brown next time)

She had long legs and a sinful, moist mouth.

He would stick his cock down his throat.

He could already feel the excitement growing inside like a hurricane of exposed senses.

The young lady lifted up her dress, she was hairy and black, slid the bracts of her dress and freed her big mammaries.

With her tongue she invited me to open her thighs, how vulgar she was, how I desired her.

I undid my trousers and freed myself from my briefs. I grabbed him like a bazooka ready to explode and saw his astonished look.

My member was tiny. Small and soft, I was minidominated.

"I WANT TO WAKE UP NOW"

I opened my eyes again in the armchair, I was out of breath.

"What a fucking joke!"

Lucid dream 24, remember ALL the details, put in hypnosis I'm a wonderful lover, the subconscious always sneaks in, now it even has irony, maybe I'm close to mastering dreams, that's why it's become more tame and allows me to enjoy myself. I can do more, I want to achieve perfection.

Francis left the PC, looked at the clock, he had been in the dream for almost two hours, it seemed like minutes had passed.

Write it down, time passes quickly, I'm hungry.

Chapter Four

Claudia finally knew.

Henry looked at her: "It seems to me that you are safe, or had you already broken all the piggy banks?"

Claudia giggled, at the American news at 10.00 a.m. the indices had all gone up, the news was positive, the stock market was going up. S&P had risen a good 6 points in 30 seconds, now it was stabilising.

"I confess that I slept hugging my pillow."

"Brava brava...for now the clouds have been cleared, if I may take some advice: phone the lawyer immediately, list your wealth and earn your fee. Then hang up. Tomorrow is another day."

"Yes it makes sense. Yesterday was peremptory, he deserves it, we don't take prisoners do we? No one has pity for anyone here, only results count!"

"I'll say it again, bravo! You are a real man...get me a long coffee later, will you dear?"

Claudia laughed this time. She was more serene now, she regretted that she had not dressed elegantly and carefully as usual. The jeans and silk shirt were not triumphant enough.

He secluded himself in the conference room. The room was dim, uncluttered, aseptic. A few Bic left in the centre of the oval table.

He dialled the number. It was the private line, he would answer immediately.

In fact, "Is she...well well, what does she have to tell me, that she knew all along?"

Claudia sank down into the finely woven rope wheelchair, unfastened a button of her jeans with her free hand and lowered the zip. She slid her hand underneath the cotton briefs.

He found her sex, it was moist with his humour.

"Of course, and good morning to you too," she sighed, her voice husky, her index finger having found her clitoris.

"Do you want to communicate something to me?" he had hesitated, it was clear.

"Yes my percentage"

'No way'

"I sincerely believe I deserve it, it has doubled its intake in just over a year" She felt the pressure in her pubis and the orgasm making its way into the mouth of her soft womb, she sighed.

"Where is he now?"

"Alone, in the conference room, no one can hear me, but the phone call is recorded, so you won't be able to retract what you say now"

"She is wicked and cunning" he chuckled "And very beautiful"

The orgasm was coming crystal clear, her breathing quickened. Her nipples clenched, she swallowed.

"I'll come in the morning to see her, she'll tell me about it verbally, sensual as she is now, maybe I could give her eight per cent."

"All right, I'll wait for her," and hung up as his index finger pressed hard on her clitoris, violently releasing her orgasm.

The other hand captured a breast, the mouth opened to gasp for air. Then stillness.

He closed his eyes for a second, the silence was heartening. The adrenalin had liquefied, the calm had returned.

The acid smell of his humour permeated his hand, he withdrew it. He got up, composed himself, washed his hands and left the room.

"The usual, right? Nothing more happening here today...do you want to go?"

'For goodness sake, standing in line, people pushing and shoving for a sandwich...do dear, I'm too old'

He took his wallet and headed for the usual bar.

Francis saw her enter before she even opened the door.

She had caged her hair into a long ponytail, wore very tight jeans and an emerald green silk blouse, unbuttoned carelessly up to her breasts.

She looked like a prancing gazelle, nimble on the heels of her pumps, her ankles thin and bony, her jeans had a small one centimetre lapel and below it, before meeting the malleolus, appeared a gold chain only worn on her right leg.

Mischievous little Claudia...

He smiled.

He sat in his usual seat, waiting for service. He put on his earphones, selected the music and absented himself from the rest of the bar, crossing his legs under the round table.

She wasn't waiting for him, she wasn't curious, she had blatantly forgotten! Maybe she thought it was a stupid coincidence, the bitch! Francis gathered his strength, puffed out his chest and prepared to attack.

"I see her happy..."

He stepped into her line of sight to interrupt the music.

"Like Francis, I can't hear, wait, here tell me everything"

He removed an earpiece, holding it between his tiny fingertips, his hand in midair, as if to indicate to hurry that it was his favourite piece.

"Do you think it was a coincidence?"

"What Francis?"

"The index is up at least five points, as I predicted yesterday in this very bar! It's thanks to me!"

"You let him up?" she mocked him....

"Yes Claudia! I brought him up and I can do it again, how can I bring him down without warning you and make you lose your percentages" He fell silent, his gaze on fire.

Claudio observed him for perhaps the very first time. The unkempt beard, the pressing baldness that proceeded from his temples as if the waters of a lake were receding due to drought, leaving a shadow of what he had been.

The insignificant colour of the eyes, lukewarm blue, covered by thick black eyelashes that contrasted with the lack of hair, at the temples and on the skull. The wrinkles that furrowed her forehead made her easy prey in a battle where nothing at the front protected her from the eye of others. Three long wrinkles, horizontally furrowing her forehead from one side of her temple to the other like the elastic bands of the rope she skipped as a girl, humming, orange, banana, melon, tangerine...

Just a little citrus-shaped nose, round and pudgy, with large dilated nostrils that breathed disappointment and helplessness.

Poor Francis, he longed to hear, how many had snubbed his stocky figure, his short legs, his precocious old man's belly?

He lowered his gaze, whispering, "I think the American stock market is too complex a decipherment for many, I don't want to belittle your advice, which was spot on, but I can't rely on it for my work, otherwise there would be no point in all those hours of study that I paid for.

Francis softened and lowered his tone, making it confidential.

"I don't know anything about finance, I'm not prepared for that. I can change reality, though, using quantum physics and other methods that I don't want to tell you about here in a hurry..."

"I don't believe in these things, Francesco, I thank you but you don't make it like this."

"I have already done it, please listen to me, can I call you Claudia? Yes I can, I dream and realise the dream in reality, it is called lucid dreaming. It took me years, but I succeeded! I dream that the index goes up, and tomorrow, it will go up"

"Well, bravo, then invest, dream and collect at the cash desk."

"Claudia, I don't have any money, but this can get me a lot of it, together we can make a lot! Don't you understand? I tell you where it will go and you invest other people's money for us, then we divide your fees"

Claudia shook her head vigorously.

"Francesco please bring me two long coffees, one to go, I don't have time and I don't take on these responsibilities, handling the capital entrusted to me! Please don't come back to this subject, otherwise I will be forced to change bars."

"You want another try? Of course, you're tough! On the spur of the moment, then if I preach well, you'll give me some time tomorrow and I can explain, OK?"

"I don't make deals with you"

"S&P will drop ten points, take cover! If it does, you will be so disheartened tomorrow that you will want to listen to me."

"Stop it or I'll force you away! You've put me off my coffee..." and stood up quickly, tipping over the shy jar of Sardinian flowers.

Francis followed her with his gaze, his mouth slightly wide open at the turn the conversation had taken; he did not want to harm her, but he needed to convince her!

She had a beautiful bottom, round and suave like two Umbrian hills intersecting at the seam of her jeans.

Tomorrow she would have been overwhelmed, little dear, and then she would have believed him.

He hoped the hours would pass quickly. He should have planned for now before dreaming.

Claudia sensed the nagging, the filthy woodworm insistently eroding her conviction.

Because inside every trader like him, there was a neat little homunculus, obsessed with the everyday. Every day equal to the next, black swans were absolutely banished and ostracised, the fear of a nefarious event in the market was averted like death, perhaps more so, because losing money, losing esteem, was perhaps worse than death.

"What's wrong with you? You're white as a sheet and you don't smile anymore...what about my coffee?"

"Sorry, sorry, I got a tip and I'm thinking about it."

"Tell me," Henry was serious, tips were essential to get rich, if right, of course.

"Tomorrow it collapses, we should acquire the put options and let the chaos lead to the purchase of the ones we have."

"That's right, we buy as much as we can, in fact, we convert today's gain, there, into put options. Tomorrow everything collapses, we break even but we have those that will be worth four times as much in a month, so we risk nothing, even if it doesn't collapse."

"Yes, it makes sense, it's very witty, and no one has to clear you, you're within the parameters agree, you can diversify assets, use strategies...fuck you're a man!"

Claudia smiled, even if Francis was right, nothing would change for them, tomorrow they would talk about it together.

"Buy Henry, buy..."

Francis had arrived home, sweet blue-eyed Brooke, she was surrendering...

He listened to his audios, imagined his lucid dream number 25.

Lucid dream number 25, I am a powerful, handsome man with the bird of a God, my space is that of money, I desire a lot of money, I can get it as I see fit, every thought I have is money, I think and what I think becomes reality. I am a God, the God of actions, all men must do what I think, and my every thought becomes reality because I am a God. I address all the powerful men on earth, the richest men, those who make the stock market work, I can command them because I am their God, and my orders will be executed immediately and instantly without contradiction!

I am ready, I get up from the desk chair, I lean back in it, I sink into it. My body becomes liquid and sinuous, merges with the skin, with the foam inside the skin, transmigrates and becomes a cell to redensify itself in another space, in another time.

I am a god, I am beautiful, I have darting muscles, bulging pectorals, toned and bulging biceps. A ridiculous skirt covers my nakedness, I gaze at it and caress it contentedly. I have long, light hair, which falls well past my shoulders, down to my back and moves in the wind like a homogeneous mass. Tattoos with Maori designs cover my body, some with pink and red colours, others black. I have no hair but a long brown beard that ends in a veiny braid.

I wear silver rings on all my fingers and a golden bracelet clasps my right forearm.

Around me there is only light, incredibly powerful light.

Maybe a sun, I have to cover my eyes with my hand, I have to be much more than normal, maybe I am as big as the whole planet and touch the stars with my body.

"I want my size to be only twice the size of a normal man's."

The light slowly fades, I see mountains, lakes, rivers and grassy meadows.

"I want the richest people in the world to come here before me, bowing on their knees, crawling on all fours because I am their God."

"I want to be three times their height and for them to feel fear, reverence and veneration."

My size increased again and stabilised.

There they appeared before me, crawling on all fours wrapped in their finely crafted suits, human worms perhaps with partially functional intuition but without having performed the quantum leap that would allow this.

So worms.

I watched them crawl, not daring to lift their heads to observe, in them completely absent curiosity and mastery of management, inside, in their souls, only fear.

'Sell half your shares, below cost, everyone! Now! Now!"

I noticed that Elon raised a puzzled eyebrow.

"We will all die, the Earth will implode in no less than forty years!"

"You are not allowed to speak, sell below cost, at half price from now on, my devotees, I will reward you by giving you your dream, any desire, another planet, immortality, boundless wealth, and you will be happy in my worship."

I stroked Trump's head, he dared not look up at me, I felt him trembling and pleading before me. If I had taken that head in my hands, I could have crushed it like a walnut, or felt its throb like the frightened robin and then squeezed and squeezed, until its bones had broken, shattered like dry sticks and pierced its heart and lungs, its kidneys and spleen. And blood had not spurted from his mouth and nose, trickled from his glassy eyes in the last gasp of life.

And in life, would he have died? If I had now crushed his square-shaped head with sparse whitish hair, in real life, would he have died?

He was carried by me, but it was not his body. It was the image I kept of him, taken from the newspapers or from television.

But the death inside my dream would have meant something in life. Perhaps he would have had a fatal accident, or been diagnosed with cancer or an irreversible illness.

(bringing a small animal into the dream and causing its death, observing the posthumous happening in life)

They all nodded off, I dismissed them, they no longer interested me.

I wanted Claudia in my dream.

I returned to normal size.

And she appeared, joyous and procubescent, sensual and charming.

"You are a God..."

"Do you like me?" I was still shy in his presence.

"Yes very much, you are sexy," he approached me and stroked my shaggy beard with his hand, first with light fingertips then with the palm of his hand.

She was wearing a transparent black negligee with roses embroidered in several places covering her nudity. I was very embarrassed. She was beautiful.

"Claudia you want me as your only collaborator, you trust me and do exactly what I say."

"Yes Francis, I will do as you ask, you will be my master, my mentor and you will introduce me to these techniques for our sole benefit."

"You will give me half of your money, of the money we will earn together, thanks to my divine intervention."

"Yes, I will do that and be honest and truthful."

"You will give yourself to me, even now."

"I will give myself to you, even now, as often as you want me to."

He withdrew his hand and brought it to the shoulder strap of the negligee.

He lowered it slowly, then his other hand lowered the other strap.

The négligé hung on her hardened nipples.

I was terribly embarrassed, I would have wanted to cover her up, recognising her power as an intelligent woman, her authority, her charm, imagining that she would never have given herself away like this, like a slut. But that her unimaginable beauty, her discerning intellect would make her a woman to be conquered, to be deserved.

Instead, an evil force spitefully pushed me forward.

I dropped the piece of cloth and looked at her naked.

She did not cover herself.

She had brown hair at pubic height, shaggy and curly, large, pointed nipples with a round rosy areola the size of an old coin. She had long, skinny legs and a small bulge at belly level, soft and crescent-shaped, which contained a small recessed navel.

I took a small breast in my hands, worshipping it.

I was a God, I could ask her not to remember anything about us, that she would only be left with the intention but not the memory.

I bowed my head and sucked the pointy nipple.

It was delicious, it tasted of salty citrus. He moaned.

Maybe she liked me.

"You like me very much, you want me to take you immediately"

She grabbed my hand and brought it to her moist sex. It was soft, with a gentle hole and soft hairs surrounding its cavity.

I took her in my arms holding her by her bare buttocks.

She clutched at me and thrust her tongue into my mouth eagerly. I felt her saliva, the fresh scent of mint toothpaste and a more intimate aftertaste of flesh and mucous membrane.

'Make me a comfortable, wide bed'

I laid her with her legs apart, she opened up again, calling me with her open hands, begging for my sex to fill her.

I looked at her, beautiful with her long brown hair spread over the sheet, her thighs open, her skin tight and silky.

The Paradigm of Vanilla's Option

I noticed that his feet were long and skinny, his ankles thin and his toes long and bony. They were still elongating, changing colour from pale pink to green.

Her ankles tangled with each other, passing between various shades of colour, until they stabilised in a bright green, leaves and stems, thorns and buds sprouted, and her body became so tangled that it merged and rose into a beautiful white rose plant.

I watched last as her beautiful face exploded into an array of pinkish-white petals, each nestled against the other to form a blooming rose, open and covered with the morning dew.

"Oh Lord!"

(absolutely remember not to force emotions, the subconscious intervened and saved me)

A small tear fell and despondently I asked to wake up.

I wanted to take the rosebud with me.

For here it is in my hands, fragrant and vivid, in the half-light of the room, in the silence of the night.

I sniffed it, I was slightly disconcerted, yet for this woman I felt a kind of shy veneration. I could not fuck her like the others, first I had to build familiarity with her. Get closer, then maybe I could. My subconscious knew that I considered myself inferior. Stupid and inferior, I would have to work on my self-esteem and our relationship to make it more balanced.

Chapter Five

"Claudia, you are a genius. The stocks plummet and you make me very rich!" the lawyer sat down in his wheelchair with the elegance of the urban man.

Claudia observed his face, carefully and taking her time to catch his gaze and hold it. He had an aquiline nose, a thick but well-groomed dark brown beard, full lips half-hidden by a black moustache and two big, blue eyes with long black lashes.

He was Italian but of clear Arab origin, his arched eyebrows both raised imperceptibly in surprise.

He was admired, an educated man, incredibly rich, confined to a wheelchair. She wanted to ask, to know, an insane, unknown anxiety seized her, she wanted to know something about this civilised man. She wanted to pay him a compliment.

"You are my favourite customer, and perhaps the only one I respect."

"Are you telling me that you don't respect your customers?" was sharp, in fact, the compliment in the ecstasy of gain and the imperceptible falling in love he was falling prey to had been poorly phrased.

"No, I respect everyone, I wouldn't imagine otherwise, but I don't share everyone's strategy or vision. To want to increase one's capital is a bit of a vague absurdity. How, with what found, why you run campaigns rather than others, this selection and how it is made makes me choose'

"So I have your sympathy?" he lowered his tone of voice imperceptibly by a note.

"Yes of course and my fear, because I knew he would come to me and scold me. My father was authoritarian and anaffective. I suffer from an incurable inferiority complex. I think I will always remain the little girl who craves compliments."

"I like her, I have always liked her. In spite of her colleagues, she is inclined, due to her feminine nature, to tell the truth."

'Women never tell the truth,' laughed Claudia.

"She is a hybrid, not a woman because she has by choice wanted to do a complicated job reserved for the male elite. And she is not a man because she is too beautiful to deprive herself of her femininity."

"Am I too beautiful? Maybe for you,' Claudia snapped.

"Come on don't play games with me, I've been well educated by life to waste time on pastimes for everyone. Let's not be all"

"OK, I won't be malicious with her. Neither naive nor manipulative."

"There now I'm curious, so what will it be? Something very distant and inconceivable"

'Simple'

"Say it again," whispered the lawyer.

'Simple and true'

A smile slowly widened for an eternal moment on his face, touched his eyes, which lit up, radiating a warm, beneficial blue light.

A hesitant silence fell over them.

Claudia lowered her eyes, suddenly shy.

"What has happened to her, why has her lower limbs atrophied?"

She could no longer look at his face, she stared at a spot in the room, ashamed. A slight pressure in her groin told her that this man was terribly attractive, that if he hadn't had two bony, hollow limbs under his grey cotton suit, she would have flirted without too much modesty.

"Why is she like that? The benevolent fate I guess decided that she was beautiful and intelligent."

Claudia stretched a smile, the lawyer's tone had taken on a warmth, these were words repeated many times to many people like excuses at school when writing 'family reasons'.

He sighed.

Her, him, both of them.

How beautiful it would have been to free each other on the table, to kiss each other with transport, to caress each other with candour.

He continued more out of politeness.

"An accident, a series of nefarious concauses that played against me and won me over."

"You don't want to talk about it, sorry, I didn't mean to be curious...just interested."

"Yes yes Claudia, you have made me many millions of dollars in one day, I will gladly answer your question, any question."

"Is he completely won?" he blushed, not knowing how to ask if his manhood remained intact.

"You're asking me if we're going out to dinner and after a heady, adrenaline-fuelled evening can I invite you to my penthouse?"

Claudia nodded her head in the affirmative.

"Would you like to have dinner with me?"

Now he had regained his courage.

"Yes, I have always liked her. She has the manners of a lord and the acumen of a barbarian, together they fascinate me."

"No dear, unfortunately I was severely and irreparably offended. The pleasure has been transformed, the innervated and sensitive areas have migrated to other receptors. Now it is the mind that becomes turgid if it lays its eyes and hands on something really exciting, pleasure has become something else. It is mental, it is in the soul. I believe, however, that you care if I can give pleasure'.

Silence.

"I get bonuses, she collects, I collect. The relationship is fair. I think that's how every relationship should be"

'Consistent'

The Advocate inhaled oxygen, his nostrils dilated and narrowed, his eyes searched hers.

"I believe it can never be fair, I depend on her to earn, to enjoy, to love. In such an unequal relationship in which only money is really the only preponderant good, I could never engage. Probably you, after years, are the woman who wants me for me alone. But you see, Claudia, I am unaccustomed, misaligned, disjointed towards relationships that are even intimate friendships. Forgive me if in front of your beauty, I rant and rave. Unfortunately, I am terribly aware that I am a cripple. But I will always be your servant, if you wish. With this I bid you farewell, even as I venerate and imagine you. I prefer it thus, my goddess, that you remain a dream' He elegantly took her hand, brought it to his moist lips. Then he let it go, lingering only a second.

"Michele!" the lawyer did not turn around, opened the door and led himself towards the lift.

Claudia felt a serpentine discomfort rising from her stomach.

He watched as long as his eyesight permitted, then walked to the door and closed it.

He might as well devote himself to the second important meeting of the day, at the bar. With Francesco.

He peeked through the window for the lawyer to get into the Bentley, waited for the driver to put the pram in the boot and then drove off.

Claudia walked towards the bar, the road was clear.

At the entrance Francis waited for her, clearly pleased.

"You and I need to talk"

"For days I have been asking you...I am glad to have your attention."

He stared at him for a second, he was unkempt, tired, heavy marks scanned his eyes. His shirt creased, his jeans ripped at the knees, his tennis shoes smeared with mud.

"I think I'm not the only one to tell you that you look deplorable."

He smiled humbly.

"I'm waiting for better times, a divorce that costs me money, a son I never see and work here that takes up a lot of my time."

"But..."

"Exactly there is a but"

'Like all social misfits, there is always a but, the desire for redemption is so strong that it also allows important ideas to mature'

He blinked, stung to the core by Claudia's disrespectful words, he could not blame her for now. Everything would change, everything would change.

He was certain.

"It was me. I know you don't believe it. But it was me."

"I don't believe it, will you let me sit down? We'll have a cappuccino and you can explain?"

"I can't now, I have to work. I'll give you an appointment, come to my place and I'll show you what I can do, my notes."

"I really don't think I want to come to your place, let's meet at a club, also near here at 10pm, finish at 10pm, right?"

"Alright, I want to be compliant, come at 10pm to pick me up, we'll talk in the car. In your car, I don't have one."

"OK, no jokes, I have the teaser."

He laughed, Claudia felt a little shiver. He was missing two molars.

"I don't do anything to you, you serve me, I tell you where to invest and you do it."

"This time it went smoothly because I know how to invest in Vanilla Options. When you told me that the indices were collapsing, I couldn't sell I would have created a bubble. I preferred to invest in insurance contracts, those skyrocket in case of default. So I split and moved the capital around."

"And you made money..."

"Yes very much"

She was satisfied.

"But you didn't trust"

"It is not my money, I am an investor for others and always rational. If I believed in black cats...you see it doesn't work like that"

"OK, fine no black cats, but I have a system that works on everything. I could make you do whatever I want."

Those words sounded crooked, Claudia took a small step backwards, her ponytail swung for her, swinging.

"I believe that if you want a partner, the relationship should be equal. I, on the other hand, have no ambition to force you to do what you don't want."

"I misspoke, simply I can make you want what I want."

"Suggestions the mind?"

"Yes, but in a big way. Please let's talk about it tonight, if I wanted to manipulate you, I would have done it already. Instead I'm interested in money, what I can earn together with you."

"OK, fine, see you tonight."

He turned and disappeared among the people coming in for lunch.

The lights illuminated the stretch of road facing the exit of the bar.

Claudia's Mercedes parked with the lights off.

Francis approached, peered into the car, she was inside, slightly nervous.

The Paradigm of Vanilla's Option

"There you are, it's 10.15 p.m. I was about to leave."

"We finished late, sorry"

"Let's not get lost in preamble, let's get down to business."

Francesco smelled of fried food and sweat, the cockpit soon became saturated.

"Do you know what lucid dreams are?"

'Vaguely'

"A kind of self-hypnosis of the subconscious imagining reality. By repeating them over and over again, the subconscious mind becomes convinced that that imagination created in the lucid dream is reality and actually replays it."

"Do you hypnotise or hypnotise yourself?"

"I have already hypnotised myself, many times, now I master the instrument, I can create any hypnosis in the dream and reality changes almost instantaneously, or at least with a 24-hour discrepancy".

"Interesting..." Claudia tapped her pastel pink lacquered nails on the steering wheel. Short, perfect nails. Long, tapered fingers, graceful hands.

"You can imagine the stock market going down and that happens. You want to imagine profitable investments and make me invest in reality".

"Yes, exactly."

"And what do you want? Money? How much?"

"10% of your substantial commissions"

"There is a risk, I invest other people's money, if I lose because of you, I have extremely strict clauses to comply with in favour of my clients."

"You are used to risk"

"Why me. Why don't you already dream of money, of finding it, of coming into possession of it, an inheritance, a legacy, money given away."

"I could, I could dream that a passer-by gives me money, if all the passers-by do that, I am rich..."

"Exactly"

"Because I am deeply in love with you and I want to impress you."

"I don't think these are the preconditions to start anything...I risk my job, my career, for your ramblings."

He was getting annoyed.

"I told you the truth. I know my place. I can do it, if you want to try again tonight, I will create what you will ask me now"

"Curiosity would kill..."

"Impossible for a woman like you not to want to try".

There was something about that man, something dreamlike and surreal, futuristic and at the same time frenetically crazy, something distant and elusive that fascinated.

"Try to bring me up Facebook shares during the day, I buy from 5.00am tomorrow"

"OK"

'At the end of the day I sell, what's done is done'

"OK, thanks, if you make money, what do I get?"

'The 10%'

"Really?"

"Yes, I am of my word"

Francis gave her a thick, viscous look of gratitude, opened the door and disappeared before she could think again.

The day had been very long, Claudia ran her two index fingers over her temples and performed small circular massages, squeezing her eyelids.

He was at a standstill, as they say.

Chapter Six

Francis entered the dark room.

Turning on the dim bathroom light, Brooke winked at the poster.

"Baby you're always cooler!"

He was succeeding, he was close to the goal. Hypnosis had to be powerful, managing self-esteem, the flow of emotions, the power of creation.

He turned on the audio of a mantra, put on his headphones and poured juice into the chipped glass.

"You are the best version of you. You can realise your dreams. You are happiness. You are wealth."

The voice in the headphones was hushed, coming in intermittent waves, at multiple volume levels and from the left and right earpiece, even overlapping. "You are entering a deep phase of relaxation. You may hear my voice from the right speaker. Or from the left speaker."

He sat down in the armchair, it was late today, he should have entered the dream earlier, he would have eaten once he was awake.

It was his big chance.

"I will start counting from 300, 299, 298 you may hear my voice now distant, part of your mind continues to count 275, 274 and part of your mind may have remained alert and you can listen to what I will tell you"

He closed his eyes, he was completely relaxed.

The image of Claudia, her carved face with the high cheekbones, the full lips, presented itself to his mind's eye. She was so beautiful.

"Let us evoke moments of happiness, remember a moment close to you when you experienced moments of incredible satisfaction, of full realisation".

She let her hair down, it was long, brown and silky like the Revlon models as they shook out their long, wavy hair and the light radiated off their snow-white faces, she let her hair down and ran her hands through her hair in a simple and incredibly feminine gesture.

You are in the dream, remember the focus: Facebook and the rise of its shares.

"Do you like me? Do you like me a little, Claudia?"

She looked at him, softly, reached out a hand and stroked his swollen, fleshy chin, taking him inside the dream, he was inside the image as himself, Francis.

I don't want to be me, now I become a very handsome, very rich James Bond-like man. I want to shake a martini in front of Claudia, well dressed, groomed, shaved and clean. I want to catch her generous gaze for me.

Claudia became suave, ran her hands over her entire body, caressed her breasts, slid down her hips and stopped at her belly and pubis.

She was sexy, her blouse unbuttoned over her breasts, the hollow bursting out of the fabric, her swollen nipples pressing against the silk. She handed me her wrists. Turned around, I could clearly see the thin, bluish veins running down her forearm.

'Ties'

"Claudia, I don't know if I can, I'm not capable, I don't understand what you want..."

"Tie me up, there are the ropes, behind you."

I turned around. There were ropes, resting on a chair. Sailor ropes, a metre long, four ropes lying on the chair in a dishevelled manner.

I took them, sampling the rough, firm material.

'I will hurt you'

'Ties'

"A part of your mind relives the beautiful moments you have experienced, the important emotions you have felt, relive them now and recreate the emotion to replay it as often as you like."

'Tie me up, I'm waiting'

I passed one of the ropes over her wrists, joined them together, squeezed, her wrists had a small protruding nub. She clenched her hands into fists, I had hurt her, she made a little grimace.

"I don't want to hurt you, I'm sorry."

"Not true, You want to hurt me"

"I want to hurt you"

"Think back to the beautiful moments of your life and relive the strong emotions that led you to those life-loving moments, think back and hold them in your memory"

I took the flap of the rope and tied it to the chair, Claudia followed me.

"Now blindfold me"

"I am sorry not to see your eyes"

"Blindfold me, you know I won't want to see"

I turned around, a black mask had appeared on the chair, the kind used for sleeping at night. I took it and put it on.

I arranged her hair so that it didn't go over her face, pulling it all back. I moved closer to do so, her smell, her perfume, was intoxicating, sweet, sensual.

My member swelled.

Think Facebook, remember your focus (remember to set the intention, otherwise the subconscious takes over)

I lingered on my hair.

"You have beautiful hair, Claudia."

"Remember the best moments of your life, and now remember that tranche is a moment that can be repeated many and many times, and just as from sleep we wake up and do not know how we do it, yet it

happens so we also wake up from tranche"

I lingered on the neck, it was graceful and thin, a small silver chain

ran across the skin. I lingered on the skin. It was silky, soft, tasty.

I sniffed it, licked a small corner of it.

Sweet.

'There's a scissor on the chair'

I turned around, there was a scissor resting on the chair.

I took it in my hand.

"Did you pick up the scissors?"

"Yes"

"Cut my clothes off"

Titubai, you are so beautiful Claudia, so perfect, you are like Brooke,

beautiful, perfect, unattainable.

Remember the focus, Facebook, the actions, you have to raise the

actions! Dominate the subconscious, dominate the subconscious!

"I have a job to do Claudia, it's my big chance, if I get lost now with you, you see understand, I can't, I waste time and I don't do what I have to...increase Facebook"

"Cut my clothes off"

"No! I'm going to go to Facebook, raise the stock, then come back to you, OK?!"

Wait there for me.

Facebook, Facebook.

Take off my clothes.

A tall histogram was materialising, I took some letters from a basket, placed them underneath the basket, F A C E B O K.

Done.

Take off my clothes.

Now let a team of masons, labourers, electricians show up.

They were as small as Lilliputians, small, all the same, dressed in blue dungarees and a white half-sleeved T-shirt. And an absurd little hat with a blue visor. There must have been about fifty of them, along with cars, vans, cement mixers, sacks of cement, iron girders.

They unloaded the material at the base of the huge histogram and began to hoist the ropes to climb the monolith.

In a short time the scaffolding was erected, they were small and very fast. I watched them, the cement mixer mixing the cement, with its continuous humming, the industriousness of those little arms, little hands.

Claudia's hands.

Take off my clothes.

"300, 299, 298, 297 and as we have fallen asleep, so slowly we return to consciousness, perhaps we feel like stretching, perhaps we yawn, 245, 244, 243"

I turned around, by now I was waking up, picked up the scissors again and approached Claudia.

She was tied by her wrists to the back of the chair, standing, slightly bent over.

I passed a blade of the scissors under one flap of the blouse, on the back. I began to cut.

The Paradigm of Vanilla's Option

The scissors cut the silk quickly. The two flaps opened on her bare back.

The bra hook divided her smooth and beautiful back horizontally.

The noise of the cement mixer reached me from afar.

The Facebook monolith was rising in height.

I could feel him panting, his back rising and falling fast.

Cut the bra.

I put down the scissors.

I placed the palms of my hands on her back and pulled the fabric down both sides of her body, shirt and bra stopped at her wrists.

I could see the outline of her bare breasts, dangling erect as they rose and fell in a tight rhythm.

Control Facebook, that's your goal, your subconscious can be dominated, control Facebook.

I took the scissors again.

I stuck the blade into the edge of the cotton trousers. I cut.

She was wearing a white lace thong.

My cock was bursting in my trousers.

You can't, don't do it, you need her, tomorrow she will know, don't do it, you can't have the certainty that she doesn't remember or that some part of her holds on to this dream or dreams it herself. She is also here in some way.

Dominating the subconscious (to be noted, absolute need to dominate sexuality)

She tugged at her bound wrists.

"Does the rope hurt?"

"Yes, do what you have to do"

"I'll set you free, no I won't do anything"

I walked around her, she was beautiful with the tatters of clothes on either side of her, her breasts bare, big, with nipples as hard as diamonds.

I cut the ropes.

The wrists had almost bruised red marks like bracelets.

He took them in his hands, massaging himself.

"I can't have you"

He removed the blindfold.

She looked at me, amazed.

"Don't you want me?"

'Not yet'

I took the scissors in my hand, they were scissors with an asymmetrical handle, black and orange.

I gripped them properly with my right hand, slipping my thumb and forefinger into them. With my left hand, I caught a lock of her brown hair; it was soft and incredibly fragrant. They smelled clean and like a newly bloomed flower.

I cut the lock and let it fall to the ground.

"Why?" She asked, surprised but submissive. Her breasts rose and fell very close to me. She was barefoot, shorter than me by about a few inches. I was careful not to brush against her breasts or skin, the anguish of an orgasm exploding uncontrollably in my trousers was a terrifying possibility. Like an excited teenager, she would have laughed at me. She would have considered me an abnormal little incontinent pervert.

I cut another lock, aligning myself at the height of the previous one.

He fell on his bare feet.

I circled around his body.

Her buttocks were firm, high, white.

I cut again. And again.

A small tear escaped from the corner of her left eye and fell silently.

"Now?"

I did not perceive regret or irony, it was just a question.

Remember your goal, Facebook must grow, check.

"Now we wake up"

She slowly became blurred, like an over-pressed photograph.

He vanished. His hair on the ground remained, bearing witness to the guilt.

The Facebook monolith had grown, the workers were still working on the iron scaffolding. They were young painters.

You can come back, remember the subconscious must be forcefully controlled or repressed, you need her. Update the hypnosis, introduce feelings of goodness and generosity.

Francis looked at the turgid bulge inside his trousers, abandoned the scissors and squeezed tightly his constricted member confined between the fabric. His orgasm came strong and convulsive, he ejaculated for a few seconds in his briefs, resting his other hand on the armrest of the chair.

Francis blinked. He was plunged into the darkness of his room, badly seated in the worn-out armchair.

On his trousers a horrible stain was spreading.

Chapter Seven

Claudia remedied this with a bun.

On the nape of the neck small locks escaped.

She put on her make-up more carefully than usual and chose a black long-sleeved T-shirt. Her wrists were swollen and sore. The large purple bruises were too obvious, in some places the skin was even abraded.

She had no explanation, had come home, taken a quick shower and then gone to bed to sleep. Alone. As always.

In the morning, she had woken up with bruised wrists and long hair just below her ears, cut as a whimsical child might do in odd-length locks. She had checked all the windows, they were still locked from the inside, the security door not compromised, the alarm had recorded no intrusions. The photos requested by email clearly showed this. She had slept all night undisturbed in her bed.

She had to get to the office early and buy the shares as agreed, that was her overriding, almost distressing thought. A kind of adrenalin ecstasy wanted her to discover that Francis was right. He could have earned millions of dollars in commissions. She would predict the future, indeed command the financial future. She would have been powerful, respected, she could have risen among the gurus of finance, so young and so female. And of course she would have been rich.

The office was empty.

He set the buy order, he would leave at the opening of the markets.

He took a risk with the lawyer's money.

He wanted to see him again.

Henry arrived later, found her absorbed in front of the monitor, Facebook registering +6% at the opening.

"What is it? What happened? You look like you're in a trance! Claudia!"

He shook her shoulder.

She slowly turned around and focused on him.

"Henry" pause, slow awareness of the power gained.

"You bought Facebook, I got the notification by email. Why? It's been going down for days."

"The black cat stopped by my place"

"Woman! Tell me why you bought it!"

"Why don't I walk under the open stairs and leave my bag on the floor".

"It's a bubble, now it's going down and at 10.00 you're left with a fistful! It was a reckless move and you put the company at risk! They teach us first and foremost to think things through, to risk one per cent, you understand one per cent! You invested a million dollars not your own on madness, on a bubble, on shares that have been losing 3.28% a day for two months!" Henry's tone was rising, as was his colour, gradually lighter and livelier. Claudia looked at him strangely, Facebook's shares were at +7.34% at 9.46 a.m. A.M. had already gained $346,765, 000 of which 8% was his.

"Sell! Silly suburban girl! Sell! Fucking Sell! It will collapse soon, it can't hold!" Henry was shouting.

Claudia's mind travelled at the speed of light, a supersonic ray evaluating, pondering, calculating, indexes, prospects, strategies.

"The black cat," he whispered.

"What THE FUCK ARE YOU SAYING! SELL! STUPID WOMAN IF WE EAT THE LAWYER'S CAPITAL HE WILL LYNCH OUR ASSES!"

"I return capital as soon as +7.99% arrives. I leave the profit in until 8.99% then I return half of the profit and leave the rest until the end of the day. I have already updated the loss limit to the invested capital"

Henry let go in his wheelchair, literally collapsed like a sack and started laughing loudly with his mouth wide open.

"Fucking hell, you are one hell of a woman, you slut! What the fuck have you done in an hour! The lawyer gets a hard-on like he used to!"

Now Claudia laughed as well, the thought that the lawyer felt boundless joy was for her a pleasure beyond sexuality.

+ 8.01%

"I have returned. Now zero risk'

"Fucking hell! What a bomb! What you buy me joy, I deserve it!"

"A Cuban cigar in the mouth of a naked, lusty pussy, her tits so immoderate you can't see the end of it"

Enrico laughed out loud, the adrenalin was overwhelming, he would have fucked even the concierge of his penthouse!

"It's still going up! What the fuck did you do to him? Wait don't go back half, just do 1/3, it fits, this goes up again, then we regret not taking a risk and at + 9.5%'

"It comes to 11 points, I know, I feel it in my virgin vagina that I can't give away."

"OK up to 10 points you keep the capital, then 1/3 and leave all the rest up to 11 points"

"At this speed it's going up it will take about eight minutes."

They fell silent, their eyes focused on the monitor.

+ 9.54%

"I have returned"

"Good, now titillate them well that you bring home a nice nest egg."

The phone rang in the tense silence of both of them. It ripped through the air like a thunderbolt or a meteor or a lunar eclipse.

They stared at each other on the first ring.

"Who does he take?"

"Your turn, you know it's him"

Claudia lifted the device.

'Ready'

'Leave capital, risk, close at the end of the day'

"No Michele, that's not wise. I'm already back, now I'm with the profit, in about 3 minutes I should reach +10 points, then I'll be back 1/3"

"Amount of return?"

"$567,000.00 at the current exchange rate".

"Remaining?"

"$348,875.00 at current exchange rates".

"And you mount them to what extent?" Claudia noticed imperceptibly that he had switched to tu.

"+11.00%"

"This you leave until evening"

'Implodes, it is almost certain'

'The money is mine'

"But I am the one who administers them, at least here."

"Claudia, leave it, you're already getting the written provision and authorisation."

The pec appeared a second later.

"Michele..." *take me to dinner.*

"You gave me a lot of fun today, Claudia, I'll raise your percentage for this operation to 8.5%, but always do as I say, at least in these areas. In every other context I am your devotee."

Emotion assailed her, biting her fiercely in the stomach.

+ 11.67%

"I came in while we were talking"

"Excellent, we agree, I bid you farewell my beautiful young goddess."

And he hung up.

Claudia did not dare look up at Henry, she knew she would read a major disturbance there.

"You are rich! What will you buy for yourself, joy? Clothes? Cars? A man?"

"Nothing...I put them aside inside some Vanilla Option, those as you know don't create this adrenaline, but they always work."

"They are like worn-out relationships, I would say, few surprises, maximum warmth."

"The lawyer says to keep the profit in until the evening. So I'm done, I'm going to get a coffee, a brioche and a juice. Shall I bring you something?"

"No joy, forget it, I couldn't swallow a pin."

Claudia walked towards the bar, it was early perhaps to find Francesco there, but a little voice told her that he was there waiting for her.

"A hot cappuccino with soya milk and a honeyed wholemeal pasta".

"Right away Miss!"

At the counter, a slouchy, bespectacled young man with a hooked nose worthy of a divinity, served her a cappuccino of soft, dense foam, with a darker core inside, formed by the coffee mixture.

"Beautiful! Thank you! Francesco?"

"Ahh you want him? It breaks my heart...he's in the back sorting out cartons in the warehouse, shall I call him to you?"

"If I can reach him, I should talk to him in private."

"What you want, pretty lady, behind the counter in the door in front of the toilet, you will find him there...but prefer him to me..."

Claudia smiled coldly, she did not prefer anyone.

She took a sip of her cappuccino and headed for the warehouse.

"Francis?"

"There he is! Claudia! I imagined it, you know. You are an honest and sensible person, you will imagine that you can earn much more."

"I was granted 8.5% commission, half as agreed is yours"

She replied dryly.

Francis smiled, a long, stretched smile of the victorious.

He was enjoying the moment.

"There is one thing though..."

And speaking Claudia lifted the sleeves of her tight T-shirt, showing her wrists. Then she slowly loosened the bun, releasing the coarse helmet that immediately framed her face made pale by adrenalin.

"Do these changes depend on you?"

Francis suddenly turned purple in the face. He lowered his gaze and searched for an indistinct point between the shameless lie and the escape, which he evidently did not find due to surprise.

He nodded his head, which could have been an affirmation.

"How could this happen?"

"I don't know ..." was a whisper.

"Yes you do!"

"You ended up in the lucid dream..."

"You took me there! You don't end up in other people's dreams by accident!"

'I didn't do it on purpose! Claudia! I swear to God! It's the subconscious, it's not exact science! It's all empirical and experiential! I was doing something else and you got there"

"So you decided to cut my hair and tie my wrists?"

"No no no ...an accident! It won't happen again I promise!

I've figured out how to dominate the subconscious... I'll be careful!

Our goal is money!"

"Mine certainly, you on the other hand are a maniac."

Francis was on the verge of tears.

"I will never do it again, I will be careful, forgive me."

"How can I master the dream, me?"

"You can't it takes years of experimentation, it's not that simple... it's

not that you sleep then you dream and create reality"

"And how is it, you explain it to me?" she alluded, Claudia would

not let go of him.

"I can show you if you want..." she began looking at him hopefully

again.

"I know you will do it again, you are rotten, your subconscious as

you call it will take you there, I don't even want to imagine what you

did to me in the dream. I will stay in our project if you give me the means to counter this, alone, it is obvious, you cannot do it. And the police won't believe me"

"Let's try to fall asleep together, I don't know what happens, but we can try. Initially maybe nothing but maybe in the long run, we could communicate in the dream, you are a projection of me but I am yours."

"OK, today is Wednesday. We still have Thursday and Friday to earn, I want to get to 1 million by Friday. You have 4 per cent."

"OK, OK"

"Tonight at your place. 11pm. You will imagine, you will dream that the S&P goes up, normal, linear as always, we play in protection"

"OK"

"If anything happens to me, I will kill you like a dog."

"OK nothing is going to happen, everything is OK, Claudia, when can I get my money?"

"They are already transferred to this Blockchain-derived credit card, you can use it on any circuit, withdraw from any ATM, convert from Bitcoins to Euros at the current exchange rate."

Claudia handed over a black credit card with an iridescent gold logo. Francis took it.

"How do I know how much money is in my credit card account?"

"This is the account, these are the credentials, if you want you can also make transfers or bank transfers."

Claudia handed over a piece of paper written in pencil.

"You don't want to leave a trail?"

"If anything happens to me, anything at all, I have deposited in a Swiss box, the story of this affair".

"Nothing will happen to you"

"You never know, the police won't believe me, but they will come straight to you and your money."

"Understood"

"See you tonight Francesco, I can't wait to try, actually."

"If I teach you, you will drop me"

"No...see you think people are rotten like you, no I won't drop you if you teach me, because I don't want to do that too, dreaming, creating exceptions cc is your role, I don't want to play it. I invest. I just need to contain you, to protect myself. You'll understand that I'm sorry to wake up with my wrists swollen and my hair cut off..."

"It's clear, see you tonight."

"Hello"

She turned around and spinning on her heels, she walked away.

By the end of the day, Facebook shares were still going up, + 15.43%.

"Shall we leave or close?" Enrico watched her. She was pale.

"How much did we do?"

"$698,392.00 at current exchange rates".

'Plus the others'

'Plus the others'

A smile crossed Enrico's face and spilled over onto Claudia. A silence full of beneficial humour enveloped them.

"We close"

"OK joy"

Claudia got up, she was suddenly tired.

"I'm going home, I need a shower"

"Sure a kiss, I'll close, rest"

He walked down the corridor slowly, heard the sound of heels clicking on marble. She took the lift and descended into the lobby of the building. Outside in the street it was already dark, a crisp air hit her face, she breathed in deeply. A hint of nausea seized her. And there in front of the street door was parked a familiar Bentley.

The door opened.

Claudia approached hesitantly. She was not ready.

'Go up'

Chapter Eight

"Lawyer I'm tired, it's been a long day...tomorrow no problem"

'Go up'

At the height of the pubis, an intimate secret contracted eagerly.

Come up.

"What happened this morning?"

The interior had the classic, unmistakable Bentley smell. Hand-stitched, diamond-patterned interiors, antiqued briar on the doors and soft cream carpets. The car's courtesy light went out. Michael pressed a button and the divider between them and the driver rose silently. It was blacked out.

It was clear that he considered his privacy important.

"Did you get a tip?"

Claudia observed him. He was wearing a blue pinstripe suit. Like the blue of his intense eyes. He wore his hair pulled back, as if he had passed his hands over and over during the day, slightly longer at the collar of his shirt. Two buttons open, no tie.

The broad shoulders, the narrow waist. And dead legs.

"Talk to me, Claudia...what happened today? You are a very sensible lady, it's not like you."

He nailed her with his eyes. A hand reached out, grasped hers. It was warm, firm, strong.

Claudia felt the saliva dry up in her throat, she really wanted to speak, but nothing came out. She stared into Michele's eyes and thought of nothing. About nothing except how blue they were.

The left was gripped, but with the right she stroked the back of his hand, lightly as if it were a tickle, her fingertips passing sinuously and slowly over the lines of his index finger, then over the back to his wrist. His skin was soft with a few black hairs on his fingers that sprouted mockingly and treacherously. They were hands that had never worked, that had leafed through books, consumed encyclopaedias, signed contracts but really had never worked.

They had no calluses, they were not wrinkled, they were soft and smooth, compact and vaguely orange-scented.

He stared at Claudia's hand, as if it were a snake on his, astonished and stunned by the intimacy.

He stopped her with his other free.

They both watched their entanglement. Claudia's sleeve lifted, it was inevitable.

"What are these signs?"

He gently took her wrist, releasing it completely, to look her straight in the eye.

"Nothing, an accident"

"Is he a lover?"

"No"

"You don't want to tell me?"

"No, not now, maybe later."

They shut up.

"Will you be careful?"

She stretched a smile.

"If I call you, will you come? If I call you from anywhere, will you come?"

Silence enveloped them.

It is always true that when it matters, words are not needed.

"Yes. For you, I will come" He gently brought her wrists to his mouth and kissed them intensely, sucking in the smell with his nostrils.

Then she handed them over to him, because they were hers, her's, even though her secret desire wanted to take them away forever and smell them at every turn.

Claudia opened the door, emotion had driven her heart pounding in her throat, she got out.

Then outside the car before closing the door, she saw that he had leaned in for one last look.

Claudia bent down, returned with her torso to the cockpit and sought his plump lips for a fleeting moment.

She quickly tasted them in his adolescent surprise, which changed to the softness and instantaneousness of that innocent lip-smacking kiss. Then Claudia recoiled in shame and closed the door. The image of him, his eyes wide, surprised, languid followed her to her car. She quickly got in, started the car and sped off towards his house.

Claudia was ready. She knocked on Francesco's address. He was waiting for her.

His house was a bewilderment, dirty, untidy, a two-room filthy loculus with four randomly arranged broken pieces of furniture.

"Have a seat, I don't know where, I don't have another chair."

"I'll get on the bed. Me alone"

He pulled, over the rumpled sheets, the blanket cover, the old ones used by the elderly, with floral prints and drapes at the corners.

"Shall we begin?"

"Yes of course, I generally hypnotise myself, I don't think that applies to you but I wouldn't know where to start with two, it's a new experimentation for me."

"Where do you put yourself?"

"In that armchair," he pointed to a worn leather armchair with a worn seat and upholstery mockingly sticking out of one corner.

"Then take a seat and let's get started."

Claudia lay on the bed, she was in a tracksuit and had arranged her hair in a nice modern bob.

She looked like a child.

"I'll start the hypnosis, put the headphones on, we'll listen in Bluetooth."

"OK, so you fall asleep?"

"Yes I fall asleep and imagine my dream, you imagine yours, let's try to imagine the one dream, which is that we build the S&P"

"OK, of course we won't be able to communicate because we'll be sleeping right?"

"Of course, you will be in my dream, to be verified whether it is you or the image I create of you, another thing. Maybe the hair will help us...I don't know we'll see. There is one very important thing to know. The lucid dream in the moment you experience it is real. The only way to know if you are dreaming is to make a gesture, an agreed action."

"OK that seems logical, which one is it?"

"Stick your left index finger in your right palm, if it passes, you're dreaming."

"It's great if I pierce myself with my finger, it's a dream."

Francis smiled, prayed inwardly for his subconscious to calm down.

"Put your attention on our focus and try to come to me. Let us begin"

"You are a wonderful person, you are a person to the best of your ability, you are the best you can imagine for yourself..."

"Sorry but what is this shit?"

"It doesn't work if you don't believe it, could you not be the sceptical, realistic person you usually are?"

"Imagine you are in a flower garden, it is a garden built within a plan that you can easily reach, this garden is full of all kinds of flowers, roses, magnolias, jasmines, and in the midst of these flowers is a fountain spouting spring water."

Francis was letting go, he was slightly more nervous but he knew he would only be in the dream, as usual, and Claudia would be dreaming hers, perhaps.

He found himself in the usual white dimension, he whistled loudly, the workers of the miniature construction company arrived, there were hundreds of them. They clustered around him, they came up to knee height, but they were for their stature really agile and very fast, at least three times as fast as a person of normal height.

"You guys did really well last time! I want to reward you!"

He pulled out from his jacket pocket, candies and sweets, lots of candies of every colour, gummy, fruit, jelly, milk, and threw them in the air, which fell like rain on the mignon workers.

"I adore you! I want to give you another reward, some money, some coins."

He pulled gold doubloons out of his breast pocket, large Spanish ones with the figure of a king engraved on one side, and tossed them as he had done with candy.

The chorus that opened at the launch was indeed one of joy and glee!

"You will do a great job again today, won't you?"

"Sisisisisisisisisisisisisisisisisisisisis"

A very quick hiss that certainly sounded like a convinced assent. In no time at all they vanished everywhere, into every nook and cranny, only to reunite under the index finger. They were already building the scaffolding.

I looked around, I was still ugly.

'I want to be handsome and attractive, a well-dressed successful man' His hands were no longer wrinkled, but smooth, his face with a beard, groomed, his hair thick and long, he could feel it under his fingertips. They were butt-length and gathered up in an Indian tail,

The softness of the chest had been replaced by strong pecs, the belly was flat and strong muscles in the legs pulled at the fabric of the linen trousers.

"Am I alone here?" he shouted loudly, his voice also baritone, commanding.

"No honey, I'm with you..."

There she is, my goddess.

Claudia advanced tightly in a tight red dress.

She had waist-length hair, intense doe eyes and vertiginous heels.

In one hand he held a rope loosely.

She is sleeping in your bed. Remember that everything you do to her here will be discovered there.

"Honey what do you want from me today?"

"I want you to take the air out of me"

"How do I take the air out of you?"

"Hang me with this. You tie it around my neck and let me hang limply. Then when I can no longer breathe, you release the pressure and lift me up."

"It's dangerous, it could get out of hand and you could die of asphyxiation."

DO NOT PLAY THIS GAME! DANGER! WAKE UP NOW!

"It will be a little something for you who are so strong, with these big muscles ..." she ran a lacquered hand over my biceps, and at the same time licked her lips greedily.

"Look, it's easy," he passed the rope around his neck and made a slip knot, tightening it until the rope was snug against his neck.

Then she threw the other end up herself.

The Paradigm of Vanilla's Option

A bar appeared two metres high. It had neither one end nor the other.

It was endless.

The rope passed over it and returned to the other side.

"I climb into our favourite chair"

The usual chair appeared.

She stepped on them with her heels. Then, as she staggered, she took off one heel and then the other, throwing them far apart. As she did so, she spread her legs uncovered by the red mini-dress and glimpsed her brown hair.

"Don't take the mmutandine"

"No, I don't wear them, I did it for you."

"Tie the end of the rope free to the chair".

I did.

My face, my mouth was at the level of his pubis.

The excitement was red-hot, my temples throbbed wildly.

DO NOT PLAY! DANGER! WAKE UP, IT IS NO LONGER HEALTHY TO CONTINUE

"Now you must remove the chair and dangle me...I will suffocate and before I die, you lift me up and give me air."

"No I don't"

"Yes you will, you yourself devised this game, it's your guilt that justifies itself, making me rather than you architect this project, but I swear it's all your own doing! So yes you will!"

"I need an incentive..."

"You see how you reason little one..."

He stroked my head with one hand, grazing the back of my neck.

With the other she lifted her skirt and freed her thighs. Then she pushed my head away from her hairy pubis.

"Lick me"

I could smell the vaguely acidic odour of her sex. She was wet and wide, two prominent lips waited moistly for me. I stuck my tongue like a stray into the food bowl and licked greedily at her humours, her flesh, her fur.

I pushed the chair back and straddled it.

I was holding her, badly because I could hear her panting. Not from excitement.

She held on to my head, when I let her go a little, she gasped and squirmed.

After a few minutes I felt her stiffen and loosen her grip on my head.

Then I promptly gave her air, lifting her up.

"Are you OK?"

"Again, I was coming ..."

I let go again, she gasped and clutched at my head, then sank voraciously into her vulva, my head exploded.

Beginning to be uncomfortable, I took the chair back and put my feet on it.

'I want more'

Her dress was gathered at the waist.

I turned her over. She had a round bottom and buttocks as firm as marble.

"I want to take your ass"

I untied the rope from the chair and passed it over the bar suspended in the air. Then I gripped the rope tightly like a leash and made her lean forward, exposing her pretty, round bottom to me. I unfastened my trousers and let out my turgid member.

I spat on it and pointed it at him like a bazuka ready to fire and started to push into the little hole.

I felt his muscles tightening, so I pulled the rope.

"Let go or I'll throttle you, open your fucking ass."

DANGER DANGER THE SUBCONSCIOUS MIND IS OUT OF CONTROL! IT HAS BROKEN THE BANKS! WAKE UP, WAKE UP!

"It is not up to me, it is you who are not capable..."

He coughed as I tugged at the rope.

My cock was losing its erection and I couldn't get it back.

I aimed again and pushed hard but the anal muscles were marble, they would not soften. So I reached down and spat on that beautiful ass.

My erection was becoming a raw, soft, withered sausage.

I let go of the rope, she coughed.

"Where are they?"

I turned sharply. Claudia's voice was behind me.

Claudia was behind me.

But she was also in front of me, bent over a chair with a noose around her neck, and a red dress rolled up around her waist as I tried to sodomise and strangle her together.

"Where are they?" he repeated.

It was her, she was the real Claudia, she was in the dream, she did not recognise me because I was different, a macho man.

But she could recognise herself.

"How did I end up here?" was another voice. From the left, again from Claudia, this one wore a black suit and wore her hair pulled back into a bold ponytail.

"Who are you?" from the right, another Claudia, also her, in a bikini with a multi-coloured sarong on her shoulders and her long hair loose.

"Idiot, the real one is me" Here she is in a tracksuit with a helmet.

There were at least twenty of Claudia, approaching me. I let go of the noose. The Claudia in red stood upright and gracefully adjusted her dress.

The noose hung like a snake around his neck.

"I always thought it licked well, I wanted to try it...isn't that a fault?"

"And how did he lick it?"

The Claudia in red began to laugh, she laughed loudly, the others joined in, the laughter was overpowering, annihilating, blaming.

WAKE UP, WAKE UP, WAKE UP!

"I can't. Wake me up. I am immobile."

Francis opened his eyes again with a convulsive gasp. Saturated air flooded his lungs. Darkness was in the room. Darkness, him slumped in the armchair and Claudia lying in bed.

He waited a few seconds for his eyes to adjust, the faint moonlight coming in through the window helped him.

She was a dark mass on the bed, motionless.

He could hear her regular breathing.

He ran a hand over his face, his subconscious had screwed him this time too. A method had to be found to dominate and subdue him, still too unstable, still too unstable.

He got up and approached her. He gently placed a hand on her shoulder, to wake her up; he was curious if she remembered the dream, if she was also in it or only her mind had conceived it.

"Claudia, wake up...I'm already done."

"What? Ah yes...ok I was sleeping..."

"Yes, do you remember anything?"

"No"

He tried to look at her neck, he did not perceive any signs in the half-light, perhaps he would be saved.

"If so beautiful..."

"I like you too...come lie down here"

Francis gasped.

"I'm dirty. You wouldn't like it."

'Leave it to me'

"I did what you asked, the index will go up tomorrow."

"OK good, now come over here beside me."

Francis thought about it for a moment, then took off his shoes and socks and threw them away.

He placed one knee on the bed, squeaked, and then the other.

He lay compressed and shy beside her.

"Finally, you are also a pleasant man..." Claudia passed a hand from his neck and drew him to her. Her tongue immediately crept into his mouth. It tasted salty and stale.

Francis did not know how to kiss, he made do with his tongue as best he could, moving it awkwardly.

She unzipped his trousers and took him under her.

Quick had shed her tracksuit.

"Take off my panties..."

"What? But are you sure?"

"Yes"

With her hands she pulled down his jeans and his rough pants, took his mildly aroused member and thrust it in.

Francis was astonished.

"Move inside me, make me come"

"I'm dirty I haven't washed...How can you want me?"

He looked at her better in the half-light, it was Claudia and it wasn't

her, it was Brooke. It was his ex-wife.

She was a girl I met on the street yesterday with a nice décolletage.

She was the morning barmaid.

It was the brunette who waved from time to time on the bus.

"NOOOOOOOOOOOOOOOOO"

WAKE UP!!! WAKE UP! Fucking subconscious! You're pissing me

off! Not this one!

He ran his index finger across his palm, past her.

He was sleeping was in the dream.

He stood up abruptly, walking away.

"Now I wake up! NOW I WAKE UP. NOW"

Plunged into the armchair.

He dared not open his eyes. Silence was in the room.

He ran his index finger over the palm of his right hand. The index

finger touched and tapped against the rough skin.

He sighed in relief.

To be noted, terrible! Finding a method to wake up quickly. Incredibly the dream possessed me, I couldn't wake up, I didn't know if it was the dream or reality. The state of confusion completely overwhelmed me.

He took his face in his hands. He was sweating, a veil of liquid oozing from his icy forehead.

Claudia was sleeping. A horrible feeling of déjà vu gripped him in the stomach.

He remained nailed to the chair, did not want to get up, did not want to breathe, think, imagine.

The paradigm dominated him. The paradigm of his existence, an unfortunate, uncouth man, unripe for every opportunity, hapless in every reality. The catch, the burden crept in nefariously even on this occasion. It was impossible to imagine a powerful, cultured, imaginative self; years of desolation, years of moral and emotional deprivation would always make every imagination murky. Every persuasion, every seduction. It was his paradigm, which he could not escape except by death.

"What happened?" was Claudia's whisper.

"Nothing!" he shouted too loud, too soon, she was at attention, already awake.

"What happened?"

'The index has gone up'

"OK"

"I strangled you"

"Ah" Claudia approached, a black figure in the darkness with blurred contours, what appeared to be an arm reached up to touch her neck.

"I'm here though, what went wrong?"

Francis calmed down. He drew a deep breath.

"In the dream, but it was a game, in fact nothing happened. You were with me, don't you remember?"

"No"

He switched on the electric light tentatively, squinted both eyes.

He headed without looking at him to the bathroom mirror.

Then back in front of him, in silence, Francis unconsciously held his breath.

"You know that, don't you?"

"Yes, I don't know why the dream derails like this."

"Why do signs show up in reality?"

"I have no idea. We stop whenever you want."

"Now I am going to medicate myself. In my house. Tomorrow we'll see if you've done your homework, the real thing. Then I will decide."

'I am sorry'

"Don't say anything, you're a corrupt soul, that's why this comes out, it's obvious to me."

"Do you remember anything? Because you were there. Indeed many you"

He took the way to the door, slowly.

"A rope tied to a red-clad, half-naked woman who looked like me, bent over like a trained dog and your limp dick wanting to rape her."

The silence was icy.

He opened the door and went out, leaving it open behind him.

Chapter Nine

The daylight hurt her eyes, she put on her sunglasses.

He had hidden the marks with a turtleneck.

"Enrico good morning, how are you? Did you sleep well?"

"Yes enough, I'm happy for you and that brings me peace of mind in every sphere."

"What about you? What's it like being rich?"

"Sleepy, a bad night..."

"Let's go straight to the office, we'll get it after coffee, shall we?"

Claudia had no wish to see others, her only thought was about the S&P and its trend.

It was 8.30 in the morning. The market opened in exactly 30 minutes.

He would have been just in time to place the order.

"You are nervous and taciturn, your mood should be something else, relax you had a crazy strike yesterday, you can breathe..."

"No not now, I want these two days to be memorable!"

"You're hiding something from me, that you like the Advocate is obvious, but I don't think it's that, rather like a secret, it seems you have information and want to verify it quickly. As if the black cat whispers to you a path that only he sees"

"The black cat... how many times does it die?"

"Seven"

"Then for five more times I will be allowed to risk..."

"What are you saying?... I don't understand."

"Nothing, nothing, please Enrico, I'm going, I don't want to be rude but I want to see how the markets open and have time to place an order."

"OK joy"

He watched her walk away towards the door of the building.

He switched on the monitors, bought in buy. He waited.

The sound of the door.

8.57 A.M.

'Three minutes'

"Sit down Henry, be quiet"

9.00 A.M.

The focus was on the index finger.

The graph marked a vertiginous acceleration, the rise of the blue line was paradoxically ridiculous compared to the graceful parallelism of the night. The cathetus of the triangle soared, formed the apex of the minute, recoiled a few points and rose again in the next minute. The sinusoidal curve of the stochastic indicator predicted two more mounds in the minutes to follow, recoiled slightly by a few points and accelerated again in the next minute.

"This I think is the best flag-raising I've seen in ten years at least!" Claudia read in an atonal voice.

"+9 points in 8 minutes"

"Tell me you got in buy..."

"That's right kid"

"You are my goddess... what do you do sell now, take home, it is impossible to continue"

"I've placed the stop loss, if it recoils, we take home 8 points of profit."

"How much? And whose?"

"You don't want to know"

"This is crazy scalping, if the boss learns it, he either idolises you or fires you"

Silence.

Claudia rubbed her neck, for a terrible, long minute she was tempted to confess. Her throat ached, she struggled to swallow and her tongue from last night was swollen and pasty as if she had eaten something stinging.

"Bring me something to drink, I have difficulty swallowing"

"I believe it joy, you have toads in my opinion that give you some thought."

"Enrico stop it, no toad, no black cat. Just reading the news"

"But it goes Claudia! Don't lie! There was no news!"

He felt ashamed.

The phone rang insistently.

It was his personal mobile phone, he was surprised, he had left it switched on.

"Hello?" he asked hesitantly, in a few had his phone number.

"I am Francis"

"Don't call me here"

"Yes I know, but I was excited."

"Stop it, see you later, now you disturb me"

'Remember me'

"I remember" and disconnected the phone call.

She was fatigued, Henry realised, staring at her brooding.

"Something is wrong, you invest as if you foresee the future, you dress in winter with 19 degrees, you cut your hair with a chainsaw and you receive phone calls during work. But not only that, you're nervous. You are never nervous. You have a peaceful character, you are cheerful and above all you are not reckless,' Henry stared at her intently.

"One stop loss was triggered, the order was closed. I had set two, the other one wider, I hold it until 11.00 a.m."

"It's not your money"

"True Enrico, true. Now let's relax, I have the trend of the 4 h stochastic, it's up, it's 9.00 A.M. certainly until 11.00 A.M. the trend is upward, with downturns, sure, but upward. The minimum and maximum points of the vertices are rising. And then every 10 cents of a point the stops update and follow the price."

"It's scalping"

"Yes, I had a tip these two days, I knew it, sorry I didn't tell you so as not to put you on the spot, let's make it easy, shall we? When I feel confident that the tips are safe, I'll pass them on to you too."

"No thanks," Henry turned towards the door, he was walking out annoyed.

"I have a hair appointment today..."

"Bravo, with all the money you've earned, you can afford a good cut."

She turned towards the monitors, S&P was rising relentlessly, her neck was aching, an email notification appeared on her mobile phone display.

Michael.

"Lunch?"

A simple word. Emotion invaded his face, his heart began to beat wildly, his stomach contracted bizarrely.

He typed slowly, "Yes, 12 noon here?"

He waited a few seconds for the answer to appear.

"Of course"

With this man, words were superfluous, like amenicules in an empty room, useless stuttering; with him, other people were the interlocutors, heart and soul. He read what was hidden and imponderable even Claudia did not know about herself. He read it and interpreted it with a vocabulary of thought. He thought, she imagined. Thought bounced and reality defined itself like circular waves in a flat water.

He wrote, "Work?"

"Pleasure"

Her nipples stood up under her shirt, she was excited and nervous.

"How much today?"

He was referring to the morning's trade on the index, after all for each entry he received confirmation from the programme.

"Very"

He looked at the small red and green histograms, they were slightly flexing downwards.

She closed both positions. She was prey to herself. Silence and a slow ticking of the clock enveloped her. She rested her head on the desk, it was cold, she felt a slight relief.

She opened her eyes, everything around her was white, there was no floor, no walls, no ceiling, no dimension. Everything was white, she herself was dressed entirely in white, only her face uncovered. A suit perhaps made of polyester enveloped her entirely, including her head, gathering her hair. She remained motionless for a second, staring at her white hands, which blended, almost disappearing, into the white of the walls, the floor, the ceiling. He widened his eyes, turning slowly. She looked, straining, around her, at the white nothingness.

Its contours almost blended into the white dimension, fading away.

"I DON'T WANT TO, TAKE ME BACK TO THE OFFICE!"

The words bounced off the white non-walls.

He waited a minute for the dimension to change, nothing happened.

A voice approached, like a modulated sound, perhaps it was words.

He listened motionless.

"Forgive me"

She squinted, trying to focus, afraid to take a step, to fall, the feeling

of being suspended was mounting into panic.

He indistinctly saw a silhouette, entirely covered in a white reflective

substance, faintly the light and dark of what appeared to be the

outline of a mouth. The silhouette was entirely confused with the

one-coloured dimension.

"Who are you?"

"You know"

"NO I DON'T FUCKING KNOW! YOU THINK I KNOW THAT

I'M HERE IN THIS SHITHOLE AND I WAS IN MY OFFICE!"

"I am Francis"

"TAKE ME RIGHT BACK TO WHERE YOU PICKED ME UP"

"I can't, I'm in your mind, your projection, your fears, your anguish, it's up to you, not me."

"NOT TRUE! STINKER, BRING ME BACK NOW"

"Remember the lucid dream is the manifestation of your desires, now you can master it and recreate a new reality for the subconscious".

She calmed down, her heart beat faster in her chest, dizziness made her head spin, she feared she would faint.

"Talk to me"

"Decide on an anchor, call it back to you if you need to return or change the dream".

"An anchor?"

Silence.

He struggled to distinguish whether the light dark in the white of what appeared to be a mouth was moving.

"An anchor" was a faint whisper.

"WAKE ME UP ENRICO! WAKE ME UP ENRICO, NOW! GO BACK TO YOUR ROOM, TOUCH MY ARM AND WAKE ME UP"

"It doesn't work like that, it's not in reality, it's in the dream...I have to go now, I love you."

"NOOOOOOOOOOOOO DON'T LOVE ME"

The tears came out quickly and disappeared into the white.

"SOMEBODY HELP ME OUT OF HERE!"

He heard a noise. Footsteps.

It was Michael, alive, him, with his contours outlined, in three dimensions.

His legs were working, he was walking towards her.

"HELP ME, PLEASE"

"It will be beautiful, you will see, now I will bring you back and we will be happy together, my goddess."

"Yes, please get me out of here," she reached out her arms to touch him and anchor herself to him. But he was incorporeal.

"NOOOOOOOOOOOOOOOOOOOOOOOOOOOOOO"

Violent sobs seized her.

"Claudia, Claudia, up you get, have you closed all positions?" it was Henry, she focused him. Bending over her, he was shaking her.

The Paradigm of Vanilla's Option

"Henry..."

"You were mumbling sleepily, darling all right?"

Claudia looked at her hands, brought them to her face, stroked herself, then ran them over her hair.

"You are not well Claudia, please tell me what is happening, I am your friend, I love you."

"Enrico, please leave me alone now, I'm going home, I need a hot shower, I'll be back by 12, I have an appointment with the lawyer."

She stood up, Henry's attentions bothering her.

'OK whatever' dry.

He got up quickly, he had to see Francis, talk to him, it was essential to understand how to master that situation to best take advantage of it without repercussions.

He headed for the bar. He was not there. She turned towards his house.

He knocked several times, there was no answer. The door was one of those wooden, basic ones, with an essential iron handle in the shape of an inverted L. He tried to lower it, the door gave way and opened.

The shutters were down, the house was shrouded in darkness. He paused on the threshold so that his eyes could adjust to the darkness.

She saw him plunged into the lounge chair, his head dangling over his body. She took a silent step towards him, watching his shoe move slowly in motion. From the toe it discoloured and deviated towards the colour white, concentric rays radiated from it to colour the scenery before her white. She stared at her hands in fear and alarm. She had no fingers, no wrists, no forearms. They were white in the white. Francis himself was disappearing.

"You're cursed, I'll kill you"

She tried to take another step into the non-dimension, but dizziness and panic made her desist. Only her face remained out of it.

"IT'S YOU! I KILL YOU! DO YOU HEAR ME! BRING ME BACK NOW!"

Silence.

She turned her face 90 degrees to the right and left, the white was around her, above her, below her, surely even behind her. She froze and waited.

"I am here, here I am" was Francis' voice, he did not understand where the sound came from, perhaps from everywhere, from white.

"Why are you doing this to me" was not a question, but a bleak realisation.

'It's not intentional, Claudia, I love you, it's the paradigm, I can only do it this way, my genes are imbued with this, from years of inconsolable failure. I must fail, my genes are educated this way. I have tried in every way to rewrite my subconscious, but I fail, because the paradigm is discordant."

"Francis, can I die here?"

"Yes"

"So I also die in reality?"

"I think so."

"Now what are you doing to me?"

"I will either make you my slave or drive you mad"

"I am your slave, it is obvious, but let me return to my dimension, take away this white."

A tear escaped her furtively.

'One thing at a time, you don't really want it yet'

"I swear to you Francesco I really want it, please, it's unbearable, I feel like I'm falling, like I'm suspended, I'm dizzy, I'm panicking, please let me at least see the floor."

'One thing at a time'

"OK"

"I like you submissive, I get hard you know..."

A gag went up Claudia's throat, acid bile flooded her mouth. She pushed the gastric juices back down her throat.

"Where you are I cannot see you, I can hear you, but you could be anywhere."

'Eat'

"What, I see nothing but white"

A white plate with white rice in it and a white plastic fork appeared in front of her, at the level of her hands.

'Eat'

"I can't see my hands, I don't know if I can pick up my fork."

'Eat, you can do it'

He stretched out what must have been a hand, as soon as he touched the fork it took on a faint glow and he could distinguish its contours.

He took a forkful of rice and brought it to his mouth.

Vomiting came up, but she stuck her fork in her mouth and chewed slowly. The rice was hot, lightly flavoured with butter, it gave off the smell of starch and steam.

He swallowed.

'Done'

"Good, now take off your clothes."

"But I don't see them and you don't see me, what's the point"

"It has the sense of obeying the command, I told you I'm getting hard, I'm stroking it, I'm thinking of coming on you and smearing my semen on your ass that I haven't been able to deflower yet."

Claudia swallowed again, empty.

Uncontrolled terror was rising from the stomach down to the throat.

"OK, I'll undress, but if you show me my body it's exciting for me too."

"You're right, get undressed, I'll let you enjoy, it's been a long time since you've enjoyed, hasn't it? With a real man."

"Yes it's been a long time, you're right," he atones.

He brought his hands up to what should have been the high-necked wool-blend jumper he had worn in the morning. There it was, he felt the texture on his fingertips, the wool was soft but light, finely woven by industrial machines. He grabbed it and pulled it over his head, pulling it off.

Underneath she had worn a sports bra, but he could not see the contours, her figure was still shrouded in one-dimensionality.

"Please, I'd like to masturbate too, if you help me, I'll take off my jeans, I'm horny, I want you, Francesco"

"I knew you were a cow after all."

Claudia could perceive the silence of his reflection, she held her breath.

"I won't fall for it, you're a fucking slut, you just want me to set you free, no my dear! No, understand no, I am not a fucking sucker, I AM NOT A FUCKING BABBLE! I WON'T FALL FOR IT, ME!"

"I don't understand what you're referring to, it was to amuse us both and besides I don't think you're a failure, on the contrary you had a fabulous idea! Even today we gained so muchiss"

"STOP IT, STOP IT, UNDERSTAND STOP IT!"

"Do you want to know how much we have earned? How much you have gua"

"SMETTILLLAAAAAAPUTTAAAANNNAAAAA STRIPAAATTIII"

Claudia's forehead beaded with sweat, panic impeded her breathing for a few seconds.

"OK, Francesco, sure."

He forced himself to breathe more slowly. He forced himself to master his fear.

Groping, he brought his hands to his waist, found in the white uniform the button of his cotton trousers, undid it. Then he took the two ends and slowly lowered them down his hips, in the meantime he breathed as if he were exerting himself after a tight jog or after lifting a heavy weight.

Slowly.

Breathe.

"That's it, good. You don't see yourself but I see you, you are so cool."

She removed her moccasins, slipped off her trousers. She was afraid of losing her balance, a white void was beneath her, beside her, above her.

She had entered the room, Francis was sleeping, but she was awake, he had driven, she was not sleeping. He was in the room, in the armchair. She was in the room, standing in the doorway and had not moved from there. She closed her eyes tightly.

White is not there.

White is not there.

WHITE IS NOT THERE.

He narrowed his eyes, moved a foot, sketching an uncertain step into the void.

He placed his foot one step forward on the linoleum floor. It was solid, it was the filthy, crusty, stinking floor she had seen a million times in that room. The armchair with sleeping Francis lay before her in the dark. Francis in the dark sleeping.

She was in her underwear, sports underwear thankfully, barefoot.

And he had an advantage. Did Francis realise this?

He observed the room in silence. Everything was still and silent.

Brooke Shield winked at her from the wall.

She approached him silently.

It came over him, towering over his sunken figure in the broken seat of the old leather armchair.

His head dangled, his soft arms resting on his legs.

She grabbed his wrist and then the other with both hands.

Under her fingertips she felt something rough that alerted her.

They were scabs of blood.

He pulled up the sleeve of his cotton shirt for good measure.

He had large, bruised marks on his wrists that ran all the way round, and in some places the skin had been abraded and showed conspicuous scabs of congealed blood.

Surprise chilled her blood and her movements.

He looked at the patch of skin that appeared from the collar of his shirt to his hairline. In the darkness it was difficult to distinguish it but it appeared as a large blue bruise on white skin, very similar to his own. As if a rope had tried to strangle him.

He turned away.

'Give him a kiss, he wakes up...' was Brooke, from the poster, in a honeyed voice.

"It's like all children, if you give them kisses in the right places, they wake up."

NOOOOOOOOOOOOOO

'I'm in the dream. I'm in the fucking dream"

She saw the white plate of rice, placed seemingly by chance on the table next to her, was still full of steaming rice.

He took it with both hands, the room was smoking white again, he had little time. He had to understand.

He banged the ceramic plate violently on the corner of the table.

Rice scattered on the floor, along with pottery shards. Two long, pointed pieces remained in her hand. On tiptoe, moving quickly away from the white, she approached Francis.

He planted the first one in his hand lying limply in his lap. Blood splashed on his face.

He wiped himself with his back. He did not move, he did not wake up.

He was back in the white, Francis was sucked into the chair, his wounded hand, the shard embedded like a pearl in the bloody skin.

She froze. Her legs disappeared, her torso, her breasts, her arms and wrists and one hand. The other remained in front of her for a second longer, a large wound deprived itself on her back, copious, arterial blood gushed out, an oblique gash opened from nowhere, gushing like a small fountain.

And slowly, in the absence of pain, the last phalanx was also swallowed.

'WAKE UP NOW'

"You know we'll never wake up again."

His voice had returned, a dark light in front of her, of imposing grandeur.

"NOOOOOOO NOT BLOODY TRUE"

"You hurt me, bitch," his voice was atonal.

"I had to protect myself, I want to wake up, earn more, do you know how much you earned today?"

"I don't care here"

"385.070,00 $"

"See now I'm interested in us getting our game back."

"OK, I do what you want. I give to you, you give to me."

"You cannot ask for anything. I command you, you are a speck, I am a God."

"OK, OK tell me and I'll do it."

The white had returned around her, above, below, to the side, behind, the co-ordinates were zeroed, she was suspended. Motionless. The vertigo was becoming unbearable.

"Please tell me. Shall I undress? Shall I put a finger in my pussy? One in the ass? How do you like it? I do."

"Yes take it all off and spread your legs."

"I can't, I won't move, I fall otherwise, I can't move"

"Get undressed first, then we'll talk about the rest."

Breathing heavily, he forced himself to slow down, inhale, exhale, inhale, exhale.

Inhale, exhale, inhale, exhale.

"There is a financial product that overcomes the paradigm of up and down, that overcomes the paradigm of failure and loss"

Meanwhile he brought his hands to his briefs, met them, cotton, with a soft elastic band, spread them over his hips and slipped them on.

"Brava"

"This product is Options, specific capital insurance contracts, specifically Vanilla Options, whether the market is in a long or short position, with Vanilla Options, you always make money."

He ran his hands down her back, unhooked her sports bra and slipped it off her arms.

"How beautiful you are, how exciting, tell me."

"With Vanilla Options, when you are unsure of the trend, you can always find refuge, so they overcome the paradigm with their incredible versatility, because everyone in the market will always need insurance, protection."

"Now touch yourself, even still, put a whole hand in your crack, I can see you."

"Whether the market has speed or languishes, Vanilla Options always make money".

"You're enjoying it, aren't you? I am, very much so, it's marble!" his voice gasped conspicuously.

"Yes of course, the only variable parameter for this incredible financial instrument is time".

"I'm coming, now I'm coming closer, I want to come on you, inside you, it would be a dream," he laughed softly.

'Time to develop interests, time to figure out how to escape the paradigm'

Francis had approached, the voice was getting closer, it was not stereophonic but one-way. And the direction was his.

Claudia cast an eye on what was perhaps his hand, in the white. Yet she felt that in her fist she was clutching something. Something important.

Francis was breathing against her, feeling the heat of the words coming out of the dark light that was his mouth. A hot, foul-smelling breath.

"You are beautiful, your wet pussy is an oasis, finally you are mine"

The pointed ceramic shard is in your right hand.

Put an end to it.

"So the first time, I bought 10,000 contracts of Vanilla Options, because I didn't trust you."

He directed the shard at what must have been his throat.

Put an end to it.

PLEASE STOP.

END.

He stabbed the sharpened shard into his jugular, blood splattered everywhere.

On the light of Francis.

His face became bloodless.

"WHAT HAVE YOU DONE!? CRAZY!"

"Sggrrrrr"

Claudia fell into the blurring, reverberating white, which was coloured by the colours of the room abuzz with Francis' loneliness.

In the half-light.

She fell naked on the floor with a shard stuck in her throat.

On that filthy floor.

On Francis's neck, sunk into the armchair, a wide and deep wound opened up. On his shirt, a red puddle swelled, fed by a small, venous river.

His body was shaken by small nervous jolts, he was going into arrhythmia.

Claudia, squinting her eyes, wanted to die with her eyes closed to stop one last beneficial image.

His fingers touched the embedded shard. Wet with his blood. Life was leaving. He had always wanted a Ferrari and to visit Iceland.

You are in a dream, now you wake up. You wake up in your bed. Nothing has happened. This day is a dream. You are left to three days ago. Francis and this putrid room and that stupid poster never existed for you. It is a dream. You wake up in your bed.

IT'S A DREAM. YOU WAKE UP IN YOUR BED. YOU BUY YOURSELF A FERRARI. YOU GO TO ICELAND.

Chapter Ten

"How long has it been since you've seen Miss?"

Henry stared at his folded hands.

"Three days and I assure you it is not like her."

The police lieutenant was dutiful but dull, a beardless boy with little experience.

"Could I speak to one of your superiors?"

"Let's get the missing persons report first, then we'll see, so when was the last time you saw her? Who spoke to her?"

"In the office, she was agitated, three days ago. Last Thursday. She was due back for a 12 noon appointment, which she missed. She didn't show up on Friday and I assumed she wanted to rest, but she didn't call in. I called her phone several times but it was always switched off. I've been to her house and she doesn't answer, she doesn't open, so, you understand, I got worried'.

"Do you have any relatives?"

"No one that I know of, dead parents, no boyfriend, no friends that I know of. She works, studies, no pets, I mean, you go to her flat?"

'Yes we will go'

"Would you like the address?"

"Yes of course, give it to me."

"Viale della Repubblica number 23, right in the centre of Milan. Fifth floor'

"Yes yes fine, thank you. Give me your mobile as well, we will try to call you."

"347984637"

"Great, you can go, sign the statement and go."

Enrico stood up, quickly read his statement, twenty anonymous lines where he stated that Claudia Minghelli had not shown up for work'.

"Sorry, I don't need you to be recalled for absenteeism but I need you to look it up. It's not like her!" he had raised his voice.

"Sir, calm down, we will do our utmost as per procedure, you can go now, we thank you for your cooperation."

Henry watched the uniformed boy for a minute and took the door.

He reflected that he didn't know anything about her, maybe they were right after all, there was no point in bothering, maybe she had met someone on some dating platform and had run away for a weekend.

She opened her umbrella and headed for the car, a persistent rain was soaking the streets of Milan. She would be back soon.

After all, where else could he find a job like theirs, so full of emotion?

Index

The Paradigm of Vanilla's Option

The Paradigm of Vanilla's Option

The Paradigm of Vanilla's Option

Finished in print November 2022

Cover price 12.50 euro

By the same author

Noi fantasmi non ascoltiamo che il nostro passato (2003)

Equilibrio liquido (2019)

Tacit assonances (2021) vers It. En. Es. Fr.

Black red white blood (2022) vers. It. En. Es. Fr.